VOL 1:
A Dangerous Life

**SEWERMEN, BANK ROBBERS &
THE REVELATIONS OF THE PRINCE OF FIRE**

**TRUE TALES FROM THE LIFE AND TIMES OF
THE WORLD'S GREATEST VAGABOND**

GUERNICA WORLD EDITIONS 85

VOL 1:
A Dangerous Life

SEWERMEN, BANK ROBBERS & THE REVELATIONS OF THE PRINCE OF FIRE

TRUE TALES FROM THE LIFE AND TIMES OF THE WORLD'S GREATEST VAGABOND

Translated by

David J. MacKinnon

Edited by Patrick Keeney
Foreword by Jim Christy

GUERNICA
World
EDITIONS
TORONTO · CHICAGO · BUFFALO · LANCASTER (U.K.)
2024

Guernica Editions Founder: Antonio D'Alfonso

Michael Mirolla, general editor
Patrick Keeney, editor
David Moratto, cover and interior design

Guernica Editions Inc.
1241 Marble Rock Rd., Gananoque (ON), Canada K7G 2V4
2250 Military Road, Tonawanda, N.Y. 14150-6000 U.S.A.
www.guernicaeditions.com

Distributors:
Independent Publishers Group (IPG)
600 North Pulaski Road, Chicago, IL 60624
University of Toronto Press Distribution (UTP)
5201 Dufferin Street, Toronto (ON), Canada M3H 5T8

First edition.
Printed in Canada.

Legal Deposit—Third Quarter
Library of Congress Catalogue Card Number: 2024933648
Library and Archives Canada Cataloguing in Publication
Title: A Dangerous Life. Vol 1, Sewermen, bank robbers & The Revelations of the
Prince of Fire / Blaise Cendrars ;
translated by David J. MacKinnon.
Names: Cendrars, Blaise, 1887-1961, author. | MacKinnon, David, 1953- translator.
Series: Guernica world editions (Series); 85.
Description: Series statement: Guernica world editions; 85 |
Works translated from the French.
Identifiers: Canadiana (print) 20240327918 | Canadiana (e-book) 20240327969 |
ISBN 9781771839228 (softcover) | ISBN 9781771839235 (EPUB)
Subjects: LCGFT: Essays. | LCGFT: Literature.
Classification: LCC PQ2605.E55 D36 2024 | DDC 844/.912—dc23

*For John Turecki, Sami-Ukrainian warrior,
body-and-soul man, who has suffered and
yet still loves the world.*

Contents

---

1. The first two long paragraphs of this piece are a prose poem, which abruptly ends with the summoning of the reader to hear a true tale about a murderer.

The Man Who Would Be Blaise Cendrars

THE YEAR IS 1904. A 17-year-old boy named Frédéric Sauser has escaped the confines of his family home near Neuchâtel, Switzerland. Climbing out his bedroom window, hoofing it down to the train station and jumping on the first train coming through. He has robbed his own parents, and has tramped his way to St. Petersburg where he toils for a jeweller. He witnesses the first Russian revolution in 1905, and then finds himself on the Trans-Siberian railway, selling coffins, knives and jewellery for a man named Rovagine. A sapling, you might say, but certainly no bud unblown, this one. More like three or four lifetimes behind him, and counting. In the *Prose of the Transsiberian*, he gives his version:

> In those days, I was in my adolescence
> Barely sixteen years old, and already,
> I couldn't remember my childhood
> I was in Moscow, in the city of a thousand and three
>   clocktowers
> And seven railway stations
> I couldn't get enough of the seven railway stations and
>   thousand and three towers

My youth was so fevered and so crazed
That my heart burned like the temple of Epheseus or
Like Red Square in Moscow as the sun set.

This hymn of a young man moved the great American writer John dos Passos to crown him as the "Homer of the Transsiberian".

In one of his reminiscences, the man we would later know as Cendrars would say: "The train I jumped on was going East. If it were going West, I'd have landed in America."

In 1911, he finds himself on a boat sailing out of Lithuania, and then, courtesy of his lover Féla, a ticket for a passenger ship sends him sailing out of Rotterdam, destination New York. And, during those lonely days faint with hunger in the New York public library, he digs deep, and from inside his cavernous mind, he retrieves the stalactites and stalagmites of the city, of the suffering of the masses of immigrants arriving, and produces *Easter in New York*, a poem that is part hymn, part beatified rap, its staccato rhythms a century ahead of their time.

He signs his name. **Blaise Cendrars**, *the man rising out of his own ashes*. At the time, Freddy Sauser has not taken the full measure of his intuition, that it was a portend of the near future. He is obsessed, with the mind-split that eventually led to the suicide of his venerated literary hero Gérard de Nerval, who failed to come up with an answer to his own koan: "I am the other." On Friday 26 January 1855, at or around 6 am, a particularly cold morning, at number 4 of the sinister Street of the Old Lantern, a man could be seen, wearing a top hat and a black suit. The man appears to be floating in the air, which in a way he is, since he's hanging from a sewer grate. A poet executed by his own reverie. Leaving another poet in his wake to mull that one over.

Freddy Sauser's solution is speed. He wants to move, and he wants to put his past behind him and clutch onto modernity. He wants Bugattis, trains, ships, speed, distance, especially distance from his past. He looks like James Dean, but tougher, blindingly charismatic. The real goods. His gaze is distant, arrogant, always on the horizon. "Step aside," it says. No "fuck you" required. Freddy Sauser is now signing his poetry with the evocative name Blaise Cendrars. But fatally, the poet is a patriot, and loves France as only an exile can. He has made a private vow: to become a great criminal or a great writer. One or the other. But Freddy is still a true believer. In other words, the perfect foil for the looming cataclysm. Freddy sees his opportunity to merge the mind split. The Foreign Legion. Patriot and vagabond all rolled into one. Perfect! Problem solved. That is, problem solved for the Generals, as the poet is tossed in the meat grinder with the rest of the suckers. Dulce et Decorum Dead. Freddy cheerfully signs up with a hand—his poet's hand!—that will soon be part of the remains of a bad day at Somme-Py.

And, then, his life journey barely begun, like all those other boys, Freddy's signature ensures one hundred per cent that he will have a big day. More precisely, September 28, 1915 on the plains of Champagne during the "grande offensive", an apocalyptic mass suicide cooked up by the greatest war criminals of the new century: the Generals, Joffre, Ludendorff, Foch, Douglas Haig, John French.

September 28. Evening, Our man regains consciousness. Neither Freddy nor Blaise Cendrars. Just a naked, shaking casualty on a road somewhere amidst the Somme-Py ruins, half concealed under a vehicle, protected only by a tarp, black rain teeming. He is bleeding to death, his arm not yet amputated, amidst legions of men also bleeding to death in numbers unfathomable. Somme-Py was an opening act, in an ongoing tragedy that led nowhere.

For a time, the man who is no longer Freddy Sauser is disem bodied, suspended as it were in the air, looking back down upon himself from the zone that hovers between life and death. Death everywhere. Death, and the theatre props for death—crushed engines of war and body parts that were intact hours previous, when dawn broke. Some of the world's most pristine and charming countryside, winding along the Marne, through the historic vineyards, but for this mise-en-scène, altered into hell on earth. Ordinary Germans and French grunts, who months earlier held pens and listened to dreary schoolmasters in villages and towns littered on both sides of the Rhine, with no personal gripe against each other, just following orders of other men, safely hidden in rooms, rulers in hand, infused with genocidal hubris.

Freddy Sauser is back inside his theatre of pain, naked. Another man approaches him. The man has gone stark, raving mad. Somehow, still following orders, he places dog tags around Freddy Sauser's ankle. Miraculously, against all odds, they are the right dog tags.

Later, more than a decade later, much has changed, including our man's name. He has been through a war, he has killed in hand-to-hand combat; he has returned from his exile with the tziganes after deciding not to kill himself, and he has lost all illusions. His first writing is a personal account of killing a German. No holds barred. *J'ai tué.* I have killed. Goodbye to all that. Vive Freddy. Freddy is dead. Long live Blaise Cendrars. Long live the phoenix. Cendrars has only one hand, and has lost his "main amie", but for the first time, his anguished soul is whole. Damaged, but nevertheless all in one piece. And ready to tell the world what he sees, through his unique lens.

Paris, France in the latter part of the twenties. A time hailed in retrospect by the *litterucha* crowd as a marvellous epic intermezzo. That would be the Americans, that is, late to the fighting, but ready and raring to throw an inflation-funded party on the graves of a million dead Frenchmen. Rent is cheap when the Generals have been flushing out up to 60,000 tenants per diem from the housing market. And, Cendrars must deal with those who know nothing of the obscenity of war, and so they presume ... Someone is stoking him, baiting him. It's a literary thing. It is unimportant who the man is. Cendrars is dealing for the nth time with a jibe from the literary quarter, sniping and belittling division. His posture and questions mark the man clearly enough and what he is thinking. Cendrars is a *mythomane*! A fantasist. He's making it all up. Nobody could have done all those things! Where are the records showing he actually hunted crocodiles, okus, tigers, boas and tapirs, had 36 *métiers*, was a beekeeper, a whaler, a film-maker ...? Cendrars' left sleeve folded up over the remaining stump of his arm. A continent and an ocean and a thousand lives separate the two men. They are in a Montmartre café and this vile reporter is feigning concern that maybe the true tales of Cendrars aren't quite as true as he was letting on. The sphinx casually executing a left-hand roll of a plain-end cigarette, and begins not so much to speak as to crick; *chicka chicka chicka*, and you can hear ten thousand crickets stridulating in a parched field. He's smiling, but it's a smile of someone who might rock this uppity bastard with an upper cut, depending on how his day is going. Finally, the sphinx speaks:

"You make me laugh with your metaphysical anguish."

The man begins to protest, but Cendrars' look shuts him up. Marking his prey.

"It's just that you're scared silly, frightened of life, of men of action, of action itself, of lack of order."

Again, the man is protesting but Cendrars is not done and cuts him off.

"... What are you looking for? There is no truth. There's only action. There's only action, action obeying a million different impulses, ephemeral action, action subjected to every possible and imaginable contingency and contradiction. Life. Life is crime, theft, jealousy, hunger, lies, disgust, stupidity, sickness, volcanic eruptions, earthquakes, piles of corpses. What can you do about it?"

Cendrars has no predecessor in Europe. He most resembles Chuang-Tzu, the rock-bottom man of southern China. An ordinary man who proclaimed nothing, and simply fished in the Pu river.

Indeed.

"What can you do about it?"

Life.

Foreword

THESE ARE STORIES from the wild imagination and even wilder life of a one-armed man who roamed the world and invented modern poetry, a kaleidoscopic barrage of images with frequent contemplative caesuras. Here's Cendrars at a field hospital after his right arm has been amputated, furiously punching the pillow with his bleeding stump … We meet his mate in the trenches who wets himself whenever a shell explodes nearby.

Here's Cendrars with the insane homosexual rapist Fébronio who has stabbed a man to death, plucked out his heart and eaten it; then Cendrars is with Pacquita, the fabulously wealthy part-Romany, Mexican woman surrounded by her homemade dolls representing the life of her country and characters from her favourite novels, *Pickwick Papers* and *Madame Bovary*.

Cendrars travels on assignment to Hollywood in 1936 and meets one of his heroes, the 92-year-old Wild West train robber, western movie maker, disbarred lawyer, and gubernatorial candidate for Oklahoma, Al Jennings. At another time, Cendrars embarks at Le Havre for a sailing to Miami. Halfway across the Atlantic, a fellow passenger, a 'trencherman,' dies and is given a burial at sea.

But the body doesn't cooperate; it not only doesn't sink but follows the ship all the way to Miami.

The effect of the stories, a fantasmagoria of the possibilities of being alive, would be overwhelming were it not for Cendrars' rhythmic, indeed, orchestrated prose.

Some English language critics have compared Cendrars to Ernest Hemingway. These people, mostly Americans, should do serious penance. Henry Miller said, "Blaise Cendrars is the man Hemingway wanted to be." Compared to him, Poppa was a boy scout.

One writer had the temerity to suggest parallels with Hunter Thompson, and not just because Cendrars was 'doing' New Journalism forty years before the term was invented. Wild living? Thompson, a bourgeois magazine writer, as was Hemingway, would have been cringing on the floor in Cendrars' convertible, a nosed, decked, and louvred Bugatti with glass pacs, two four-barrels and two Samoans, three showgirls, and a pair of lepers in the back seat.

If this sounds like Big Talk, read these stories and then tell me about it.

Introduction

ONE OF THE most enjoyable things in life is to come across a writer whose words strike a chord, someone who tells about places and situations you've never encountered before and whose perception of life is vastly different from yours. It becomes even more gratifying when such a writer has lived a remarkable life and writes using what was once known as "muscular prose.

Blaise Cendrars' prose is characterized by its striking boldness and natural flow, which can leave the reader in awe of its sheer directness and forcefulness. At times, it can even be described as stunning, leaving an indelible impression on the reader's mind.

Cendrars led an extraordinary life. His stories tell of adventures on land and sea and in some of the world's least hospitable places, such as a Brazilian prison, where he encounters men who have done terrible and violent things. Or in mining camps, where desperate men and women scratch out a meagre living against a background of greed, corruption and violence. Or aboard a sailing vessel, where the exploits of a drunken cook and his treasuring of a particular coffin have surprising consequences. He has met some astonishing characters, as the reader will soon discover.

Cendrars served as a French soldier in World War I, where he lost an arm. His writing about the war and its cruelty and inhumanity is terrifying. He evokes both the madness of the massacre, the sordid and unhappy lot of the foot soldiers, as well as the simple acts of humanity that typified life in the trenches. His first-hand account of the First World War stands equal to the writings of Robert Graves, Sigfried Sassoon, and Erich Maria Remarque.

Kurt Vonnegut somewhere comments that there are two types of writers. The first is the literary kind, which draws inspiration from other writers and the vast storehouse of literature. The second sort of writer draws inspiration directly from life. Vonnegut adds that neither type is superior, and most writers are of some hybrid formation.

But Cendrars is assuredly a writer of the second kind. His stories are taken directly from his lived experiences and have the authenticity and verisimilitude of a man who has witnessed extraordinary things. They occupy that odd space between journalism and fiction, the same literary genre which, many years later, after the publication of Truman Capote's *In Cold Blood*, became known as "non-fiction novels." Cendrars was well ahead of his time. His narratives can be accurately described as "non-fiction short stories."

When David MacKinnon, the editor and translator of this volume, asked if I could lend a small hand in editing these tales for an English-speaking audience, I jumped at the chance. Blaise Cendrars was a name I had heard, but that was all. I knew he had a devoted readership in the Francophone world, but I knew nothing of his work or life. Editing these new translations was a chance to familiarize myself with a highly regarded writer whose work was unknown to me. I now count myself among his fans.

I hope these stories will find a wide readership in the Anglophone world. Cendrars is anything but politically correct. He writes about men and women honestly and tells us of times and places far removed from our own, with very different sensibilities and understandings of the world. Crucially, he was writing at a time when a writer was expected to be a truth-teller rather than a propagandist for the ideological flavour of the month. What strikes the reader most forcibly is the unmistakable ring of truth that emerges from his pen.

Cendrars stands in stark contrast to a pernicious contemporary development that would reduce literature to a mere programmatic tool for bolstering political dogmas. He is no mere propagandist. These tales do not transmit clear and simple moral messages. Even less are they an apology for a political ideology. Instead, he explores complex and nuanced themes so that we, as readers, are able to feel deep empathy towards even the most flawed or villainous characters. These stories remind us that art and the aesthetic experience are not about confirming and reinforcing our existing beliefs. Instead, authentic aesthetic engagement involves encountering diverse perspectives and gaining new insights about the world. Cendrars' writing demands creative and empathetic thinking, which Kant calls "disinterested contemplation"—a vital element of the aesthetic experience.

The critic Stanley Cavell once remarked that the study of philosophy is an education for adults. It is a pursuit that requires us to let go of our juvenile preoccupations and confront the complexities of the human condition with honesty and openness. The same can be said for Cendrars' stories, which offer us glimpses into both the wonders and depravities of human life.

Blaise Cendrars' opus merits becoming part of the ongoing conversation in the English-speaking literary community. And I think this is particularly important at this cultural moment, when what has aptly been called the "woke mind virus" has captured and colonized much of the Western imagination. Too frequently, writers in recent years have been defenestrated by the morass that is political correctness, with its so-called "sensitivity readers," humourless court eunuchs, and a censorious audience ready to pounce on any sin against the Church of Wokeness. He is a breath of fresh air in his celebration of an uncommon life lived to the full.

For those who are new to Cendrars, I bid you a hearty welcome. You are about to enter a world unlike yours, populated by fabulous characters and wondrous tales. It is a world far removed from our own—but one well worth the visit.

PATRICK KEENEY
Hua Hin, Thailand

FÉBRONIO
(Magia Sexualis)[1]

PRE-ORIGINAL PUBLICATION under the title "A Penitentiary for Blacks" in *Paris-Soir*, 30–31 May, 1–2 June 1938. On the 30 May front page, a leader introduced the interview:

> *The powerful, brilliant author of* Gold, Moravagine, Rum, Dan Yack, *is also—and our readers know this better than anyone—a journalist of the first order. Today, we commence his extraordinary report on the famous Black penitentiaries of Brazil. Blaise Cendrars is the sole journalist who has succeeded in visiting these prisons, where he came face-to-face with the most deviant of Brazil's serial murderers. His story is brief but infused with strength, insight and humanity. It falls within the pure tradition of Cendrars'* True Tales, *published in* Paris-Soir *and recently compiled into a single volume containing some of the greatest works of a legendary writer.*

---

1. Conselheiro Antonio Prado was the father of Paulo Prado. This dedication replaces, on later drafts, a dedication "to madame Eugenia Huici de Errazuris," the great Chilean friend of Cendrars.

1

Because it was presented as reported, the tale provoked protests among Brazilians unhappy with the image conveyed of their country, so vociferous that it triggered the following preface to the June 1ˢᵗ issue:

The hallucinatory reporting of Blaise Cendrars has triggered a strong wave of emotion in the Brazilian colony of Paris, our reporter has informed us:

> *"In every era and in all countries, humanity has seen emerge from its own ranks, the emergence of monsters: Jack the Ripper in England, the Dusseldorf vampire in Germany, Landru, Weidmann in France, not to mention Gilles de Rais, the Bluebeard of Legend/Doctors, lawyers, coroners, psychiatrists, priests, but also writers study with anguish these monsters, enigmas of the human soul./But I am unaware that I have lacked respect or love that I hold for Brazil, for if every man has two countries, his own and France, every Frenchman who knows Brazil also has two: France and Brazil."/Blaise Cendrars*

I
The Prisoner with the bouquet of Violets

What most impressed Albert Londres[2] when I brought him to visit the Rio de Janeiro penitentiary was the happy-go-lucky atmosphere of insouciance, freedom of movement and virtually unbridled autonomy reigning inside the penitentiary. I could see he was fairly taken aback as I watched him emerge from the car while I prepared to show my entry pass and authorized visit permit to the guards. The

---

2. Albert Londres (1884–1932) French journalist considered as the father of French investigative journalism. This lightly ironic portrait allowed Cendrars to position himself as a special correspondent by portraying himself as the guide for his prestigious but naïve colleague.

special correspondent was greeted by the commotion and fanfare of a band, the raucous shouts of joy of a delirious mob, the thuds of a soccer ball, while the squeaking and scraping of mandolins and violins were audible from the other side of the prison walls.

"What the hell is going on here, an evening gala event?" asked Albert Londres. He was, to say the least, intrigued. "Where are you leading me, Cendrars? I was preparing myself to visit a moribund, dreary penitentiary, and this looks more like a neighbourhood feast or a sporting gala, but it's hard to tell which. Nobody here looks too crushed by their existence. They even look like they're enjoying themselves. So, this is what you call a model prison? It's incredible. Surreal, even. It's crazy."

On that note, we were ushered through. The guards opened the last gate, and we found ourselves inside the prison yard, brimming with hundreds and hundreds of prisoners, hanging, snapping their fingers, gambling, gabbing, gambolling about in complete liberty. Albert Londres burst into laughter.

"C'mon admit it Cendrars, this is crazy. I come all the way from Rio to find Dieudonné, and you promised me that I'd be visiting the dark cell where the federal authorities had, up until the last few days, held under lock and key the famous convict of the Bonnot gang, the escapee from Guyana. I thought I would have the readers of the Petit Parisien shaking in their boots by describing to them the horrors of the House of the Dead. And then you bring me to see a fair, a show worthy of the famous carnival of Rio. Ah, Brazil! What a country! ..."

He was right. The yard was teeming with convicts, and in the midst of this dense mob, Blacks were pulverizing a soccer ball, sending it whirring into the air, then spinning and whirling earthwards, bouncing with a thud on the pavement, welcomed as it were by a cacophony of horns, bass, kick and snare drums, fifes, and a motley range of percussions belting out a raucous cacophonic fanfare. The music looked to be blasting our way from over the rooves of a second yard, where the prison musicians were executing a diabolical *maxixe* dance, only to launch non sequitur into a solemn rendition of a patriotic hymn. The spectators acclaimed the soccer virtuosos to the echoes of music lovers clapping to the music or joining in on the refrains. At all the windows of a five-or-six-storey façade, pairs and trios of other Blacks playing guitar, viola or flute, singing, whistling, laughing, wriggling and jiggling, foot-stomping and beating time.

This hullaballoo was as raucous in every yard, and far from interrupting or distracting these performers, our passage through only succeeded in ratcheting up the din. Albert Londres no longer knew what to make of this prison. The few old convicts, the straggles of solitary figures, the odd and rare appearance of hangers-on who came to escort us as we moved from one yard to the next, chattering, shouting spontaneously to their friends in captivity, offering us small works to sell or to exchange—sculptures made with their knives, pyro-engraved belts, dolls carved out of mahogany, wickerwork, musical instruments in tortoiseshell-carved ornaments of dancing girls and women in raffia. They were in no way rendered claustrophobic by their imprisonment and responded most courteously to each of our questions. And they weren't inhibited in the least by the presence of an official who accompanied us.

"You don't know Brazil," I said to Albert Londres. "You have no idea about this people, especially ordinary Brazilians, whose natural goodness, innocence and indolence are legendary as is the insouciance you can detect if only you listen to their music. It's probably in part due to the climate, in part due to the mix of bloodlines ..."

But Albert Londres' stupefaction appeared to have paralyzed him. He noted with astonishment that all these men were smoking large, stalk-cut wrapper cigars. The crowd was dressed very respectably in whites and well-washed denim. Come to think of it, none of these convicts were clad in the drab gear of the convict. Pretty well any way you looked at it, a good number of the prisoners appeared to be doing very well. Card games were actively underway everywhere under the arcades, as were other gambling and skill games. I observed to him that there were solely coloured people in the penitentiary, Blacks of every range of the spectrum and every type, ranging from the prognathic Congolese to the Indian Metis sugar-loaf skull, and every possible degrading tint, from the charred kettle-bottom to the unripe, emerald-lemon yellow to faded saffron, to sepia, to violet cinnamon, to withered blotting-paper skins to glistening tar to asphalt blue.

"How many of them are there, you ask? Two thousand? Three thousand? Listen up, my dear Albert Londres; every last one of them is an assassin."

Still, there was more in wait for Albert Londres, who was already getting a full dose of stupefaction and astonishment, was agape to learn most of these cold-blooded murderers, unless they were serial killers or mentally deranged, each enjoyed periodic day-passes to stroll free about town.

"What do you expect, my friend? Look at this tincture of blood. Add on the burning Rio climate and their exuberant nature, and it's not hard to understand that every last one of these men would go off the deep end if they weren't allowed a little side-trip into town from time to time.

The official accompanying us sided entirely with me, but Albert Londres remained incredulous.

"And, of course, they all actually return at day-end?" he asked.

"Not only that. They all arrive on schedule. Never a single one missing."

"This doesn't make any sense!" protested Albert Londres. "Come, tell me, if they can all go into town, why wouldn't they fly the coop?"

"Because these negroes are good Christians," I chimed in. "They have killed, and they're paying the price. But if they were brought to the point of killing, it has always been on points of honour. There's nobody more tetchy and jealous than these Blacks who simply cannot pardon an insult. Either they had to settle an old family vendetta or exterminate members of a rival clan. These aren't vile assassins. You might have noticed there isn't a single White among the lot."

The prison warden had recommended to the turnkey who was charged with our visit to open all doors and gates upon request, satisfy our every desire, invite us to dig around wherever we liked, and hide nothing from us. As he informed us, he had no desire to leave a famous French special correspondent with the impression that there were any mysteries or secrets to hide. It allowed Colonel Alfonseca to display his liberalism and pay homage to Albert Londres' investigations, which he had already read in-depth. I recall, when crossing a lower chamber in an old building, the sole remaining vestige of the old regime in the ultramodern Rio de Janeiro penitentiary, a dark room with what appeared to be oversized crates made of wood leaning against walls. These were odd pieces of furniture to stumble across in such a location, and Albert Londres initially took them to be rabbit hatches. I forced open these suspicious-looking chests of drawers, and voilà! Three naked men emerged, huddled up in these hermetically closed boxes. Three madmen.

"At last!" said Albert Londres to me. "Now, we're getting somewhere. You'll not deny it—this has more the whiff of a penal colony!"

He turned to the guard, asking: "Why are these men shut off inside there, tell me?"

I was serving as an interpreter between my colleague and our guide. I felt deep embarrassment, almost a sense of shame to discover that the three naked men were Whites, a fact that Albert Londres seemed to have completely overlooked in his spiteful triumphalism at exposing a wrong of the administration.

"It's to keep them calm," responded the guard blithely.

"Then, why are they naked?"

"Because they tear off their clothes when they're throwing fits."

"Fits?"

"Delirium tremens. These are alcoholics."

"I see. And is this frequent?"

"That depends. Once or twice every three months."

"You don't have any straitjackets, obviously, since you're locking them up in these wooden crates?"

"They haven't arrived. We have ordered them from the United States."

"And do you have quite a few of these oddballs?"

"No, just these three. They're foreigners that the Rio climate and the promiscuity of the negroes drives to distraction and demoralizes."

All three had been convicted of heinous crimes, and I had surmised correctly. They were the only three white men we spotted throughout our visit. Two were English, both of them human wrecks. The third was a Norwegian sailor, an animal—like I say, human flotsam.

* * *

I still recall that when we were inside the empty cell of Dieudonné[3], a seared remnant of a man as ravaged as Moravagine entered the cell, interrupting Albert Londres, who was still painstakingly taking measurements, to offer him a bouquet of violets.

This was the dean of the penitentiary, the longest-incarcerated inmate, known as the "convict with the bouquets of violets." I had already heard a fair bit about this man.

He was serving the maximum sentence for his crime, which had been committed in a raging outburst of jealousy. He not only harpooned his rival but plucked out his heart, gnashing it to shreds until he had completely devoured it.[4] For twenty-two years, this homicidally jealous case was denied parole. For twenty-two years, this maniac cultivated—one can only imagine the dark passion he infused into his obsession under this fiery climate—violets in the corner of a covered section of the prison yard.

He was a mulatto fisherman, a Navy deserter, who I think was native to Jurujuba, a Polynesian hamlet tucked away somewhere off

3. In 1927, Albert Londres travelled to Brazil to meet Eugène Dieudonné, convicted as the accomplice of the Bonnot gang who had succeeded in escaping from the Cayenne penal colony. He recounted his adventure in *L'Homme qui s'évada* (1928) and managed to have him rehabilitated. This context allows us to approximate the date of the meeting of Cendrars with Fébronio as having occurred in 1927.
4. For another similar case, see *Eloge de la Vie Dangereuse* (In Praise of the Dangerous Life) (cf Blaise Cendrars: *Aujourd'hui*, 1 vol. Grasset 1931; and the most notorious case in History, that of Don Pedro, Pedro the cruel, tearing out with his teeth the heart of his father's counsellors, who had obtained from the late king the right to execute his lover, the celebrated Dona Inès (cf Antero de Figueiredo: D. Pedro et D. Inès, 1 vol., Livraria Bertrand.Lisbon, s.d.).[Note of B.C.]

the coast of Rio. He informed me that his name was Gabriel Pequeno. He had an anchor tattooed in the palm of each hand, and the violets he offered bloomed double flowers and were gigantic.

However, after twenty-two years of incarceration, this little scrap of a man still hadn't forgotten anything, and when I spoke to him of his hideous deed, he immediately said he'd go right back to his old ways.

"She was that beautiful, your *mulatinha*?" I asked.

"Oh! Marie-des-Anges? She was my heart."

"And you can't get your mind off her?"

"No, because you only have one heart, only one."

And this cursed soul turned on his heel, shuffling his way between the prison cages.

II
Fébronio Indio do Brazil

Each prison has its own monster. At the time of our visit, the Rio de Janeiro penitentiary had caged (while waiting to assign him with the criminally insane, where this perverted serial killer has been incarcerated since 1927[5]) a sadistic monster whose crimes and vertiginous folly had terrified the public. Month after month, the newspapers devoted their pages to Fébronio Indio do Brazil, "the Son of Light," as the Negro madman, who extracted the teeth of his victims and tattooed them with a cabalistic sign, referred to himself. So, I set out to pay a visit to Fébronio. But our guide caused me no end of difficulties. Even more so than Albert Londres, who was utterly ignorant of the doings of this ritualistic assassin. So, after measuring the

---

5. "1926". When Cendrars landed in Brazil in 1927, the population of Rio was terrorized by the serial crimes of Febrônio (which Cendrars had transcribed into Fébronio) who, once arrested, would spend the remainder of his life in prison where he would die an octogenarian (he can be seen in a documentary filmed in 1981). Cendrars, the author of *Moravagine*, clearly believed that, in Fébronio, he had discovered the reincarnation of his diabolical double.

empty cell of Dieudonné, which was no bigger than a doghouse, he had fulfilled the purpose of his visit. He had already been showing signs of impatience and, from one minute to the next, rushed out on the pretext that it was time for his daily cable sending.

Having completed a brief call of my own to Colonel Alfonseca to confirm my authorization to visit Fébronio and after a quick adieu to my compatriot who was leaving in the company of our first guide, I was escorted by two armed guards and a new turnkey into the high-security section where the most dangerous criminals were held in total solitary.

The *confino* resembled a deserted menagerie. Alone in the large central cage, a small, naked negro, with sculpted Herculean musculature was seated on the ground stoking a fire he was tending to, adding straw from his bedding stalk-by-stalk and newspaper pages that he twisted and torqued like rags before tossing them into the flames.

He was plunged deep in a profound meditation, utterly oblivious to our arrival. I walked up to his cage and pressed my head against the bars to better make out the silhouette of his traits in the shadows and give him a better sight of me.

"Fébronio, I'm coming … Fébronio!" I shouted.

"Sir, watch out!" growled one of the guards, who kept a good three paces behind me while another kept his hand firmly gripped on his revolver. "Be careful! Don't approach him! The devil could strangle you! He's a monster and strong as an ape."

"I'm not so sure!" I said. "Fébronio won't hurt me. I know him. I've read his story in the newspapers. He's not the devil you take him for. This is a man who obeys, who hears a voice, who is submitting. He says he has a mission. I take him at his word …"

I slipped my hand through the bars as if getting ready to tame a cat: "Fébronio!" I called out again. "Fébronio, have you heard what these ones are saying about you? But I'm sure of it. You're not the devil they say you are, are you? … Listen, Fébronio, I come from France and want to talk to you. I'm not with the police. I write for the newspapers. Not the local papers, the Paris press … Ever been to

Paris, Fébronio? … Heard about it? … Well, listen to me, Fébronio, your story intrigues me. I don't wish you any harm. All I want to do is talk to you …"

For a good quarter of an hour, I called out to Fébronio in this manner, without the naked man acknowledging my presence other than pivoting on his buttocks, showing his backside to me.

"That's more than enough," one of the guards growled. "You've had your sighting of this dirty nigger. Time to go."

But I wasn't done. "You don't want to talk to me, Fébronio? … Have it your way. Listen … I won't overstay my welcome; I'll ask you a single question. You wrote a book, didn't you? *The Revelations of the Prince of Fire*[6] … That's it … So, tell me, where can I find a copy? I've been looking for it in all the Rio bookstores, but nobody seems to know your book. So, what do you say? Would you lend me a copy so I can read it? I've written a book or two myself …"

A harrowing minute of suspended anguish passed. Suddenly, Fébronio sprang up, leapt across the dirt floor and sprang onto the bars like a big cat.

"The bastards," he bawled. "They beat me, the *macaques!* They wanted my book, but I wouldn't cough it up. Today, I learned through the investigating magistrate that they found it, and the police burned my book. Ah, the low cunts! The *macaques!* …"

The guards had leapt backwards and were cowering. Fébronio continued hissing out rabid curses. I could feel the heat of his feverish breath gusting across my face. Our faces were only separated by the bars of his cage.

"Oh, my friend, my dear, dear friend …" the negro murmured, panting and heaving. The strangler's fingers gently stroked the back of my hand.

---

6. Fébronio's book, *As Revelaçoes do Principe do Fogo (The Revelation of the Prince of Fire)* seized and destroyed by the police, had for a long time been considered as lost until Carlos Augusto Calil recently discovered a copy in the library of the writer Mario de Andrade. An excerpt was translated and published in *Brésil, l'Utopialand de Blaise Cendrars (Brazil, the Utopialand of Blaise Cendrars)* (Maria Teresa de Freitas and Claude Leroy ed. L'Harmattan, 1998, pp 157–161.

* * *

I offered him cigarettes, but Fébronio informed me that he neither smoked nor drank.

His nerves had settled. I remained an hour with him, and he was utterly docile and charming.

His elocution was expansive yet rhythmic. He tended to drift when it came to minutiae and then to come back and correct the details. A certain dream-like lethargy was operative, even a reluctance to leave off one topic for another.

This man was beyond a shred of a doubt obsessional. The only thing I knew of him I'd read in the newspapers. Watching his feline mannerisms, his supple gestures, the rippled waves of his hair, his silky goatee, and his fleeting smile, that upon hearing a word could naively illuminate his entire face and alleviate the profound sadness locked in the obscurity of his gaze, I found it hard to believe I was in a tête-à-tête with a blood-thirsty madman, and my mind continually raced for avenues to satisfy my curiosity without triggering his ire.

This brute had admitted his guilt of the most heinous crimes without batting an eyelid. The depths of his soul were troubled, he explained. He had been beaten, rumbled by the devil, manhandled by no other than Satan himself. This forlorn soul explained how he had been forced to act, to obey his fragmented visions and the voices that invaded his spirit from the heavens. He was a ferocious beast, revelling at the recollection of basking in steaming entrails, barking and lapping up the blood. This killer could no longer reckon the number of his victims and had no awareness of the enormity of the abomination of his deeds. At the same time, this inhuman sadist had no external mark of bestiality, nor any hint of a physical defect, except perhaps the lobe of the left ear, pinned to his skull, and maybe also his cavitied teeth, a repugnant trait, particularly in a negro and which triggered a physical revulsion. Something withered, condemned, obscene had been externalized on his face.

He was well-proportioned, had lovely musculature, and was very male. On his well-endowed torso, he bore the tattoo of an initiate:

EU SO FILHO DA LUZ
(I am the Son of Light)

And on the folds of his belly, the two flanks and in the back, the size of a palm and engraved in double, capital letter font, the fateful inscription:

D.C.V.X.V.I.

This was the cryptic message that this unhinged, autodidact dental surgeon tattooed on the innocents that fate cast upon his path—the prophetic portend of the new religion, the first leader of which was none other than Fébronio himself, as he proclaimed. The religion of the Living God, to be imposed by the law of violence! (*"Deus-vivo, ainda que com o emprego da força!*)

* * *

The criminality of coloured people, or even primitives, who are in daily contact or in the grip of modern civilization and who have more or less, willingly or by force, submitted to, adopted, imitated, rote-learned, aped, and often to the point of inhibiting their most natural instincts and reflexes, the mentality and the prejudices of their white masters and bosses, has always drawn my curiosity as I consider this as a short-circuit, a reflective flashback, a backlash.

In Brazil, for example, the *metissage* of races is a deeply rooted and ongoing process. In the past, the Portuguese pioneers of the 16th century mixed their bloodlines with imported negresses and Indians whom they ravaged and where their descendants and heirs intertwined with each other by multiplying patriarchally right up until the emancipation of the slaves, which only dates back to 1887. This general cross-pollination was then succeeded by other strains during modern times: an initial wave of Mediterranean settlers, substantial Nordic immigration and, over recent years, a large contribution of the Yellow Races. Is it surprising that within this tropical country, the criminal annals exceed in every way the complexity, oddity, and original and aboriginal mentality they reveal: an enigma of the human soul that disconcerts psychiatrists and specialists?

Shortly before the explosion within Rio of the sensational affair of Fébronio Indio do Brazil, another crime had taken hold of the public mind. That of a Japanese man, who in a paroxysm of terror—mystical terror or ancestral terror—had executed his entire family, presented a troubling enigma to the public of Sao Paulo.

I am speaking of the massacre—or of the holocaust, if you like—of Pennapolis that remains unfathomable.

Kadota was a poor Japanese settler, one of thousands in the township of Pennapolis. This hamlet is dominated by an immense orchard of lemon and orange trees, mandarin trees and cedars, avocado and mango plants. It is subdivided into well-tended plots by methodical Japanese gardeners who worked day and night like ants, meticulously and with stubborn perseverance such that at 10,000 kilometres from their fatherland, they succeeded in cultivating a few tea plantations and rice paddies. This conferred upon this corner of the great Sao Paulo suburbs—which are generally abandoned and lacking in features—the refinement of a Japanese woodblock print, a classical miniature valley with its earthworks, its lakes and canals, and its diminutive, barely discernible crescent-moon bridges.

Through work, perseverance, privation and the meagre savings he had scraped together over the years, Kadota became the owner of the parcel he cultivated. He had even managed to procure a Ford pick-up to deliver fruits and vegetables into the city, which was all part of his plan to open an account in a capital city bank soon.

Kadota had taken eighteen years to acquire this patch of prosperity, and he had every reason to be proud. Hadn't he succeeded in bringing his wife Touki and her firstborn to live with him? And were his three other sons not born on this land, in this small fazenda of Aqua Limpa, which today was finally his property?

All his compatriots admired Kadota's success, and his neighbours envied his good fortune.

Then, an ill-wind arrived one night in May. It was the rainy
season. Since the onset of the rains, the new owner had been confined to his home in a state of enveloping anxiety, taciturn, starting
at each gust of the wind, brooding, expecting misfortune, imagining
that he was being staked out to steal his goods or to murder him all
because of the Ford that was his pride and joy, and paradoxically, the
public manifestation of his wealth brought with it the fear that a
terrible event would take it all away. During one of these nights,
when Kadota couldn't sleep, the ascendant terror broke him. He
woke up his wife and his four children, ordered them to lay on the
ground in order of size, his wife at the extreme right, near the
hearth, his last-born on the far left, nearby the door, and he slit their
throats in sequence, commencing with the youngest, a nine-year-old,
then the third-born, who was 11, then the second, who was 14, and
finally the eldest, who was 17, and ending the serial massacre by the
mother, the faithful, the valiant, the obedient Touki, who was 34
years of age. Then he excavated his stash, wiped off his knife, and
Kadota started up his little Ford, the source of his vain pride, and
drove down to the police station.

When this afflicted Japanese man, who until that very moment
had been diligent and a model settler, was asked how he possibly
could have come to this, Kadota responded mechanically that he
had been confined to home for days. It was the rain. That was it.
The rain that simply wouldn't let him be. Until sleep came to an
end, the din of the wind howling through the Eucalyptus. Then,
due to his certainty of lurking murderers and thieves, the night previous, he had already had a fright. That was when the Vision
appeared before him ... an old man, a horrible, wrathful old man,
who ordered him to wake up Touki and his four sons, Taro, Jiro,
Saburo, and Shiro, and to lay them out on the ground and to sacrifice them.

Later, they succeeded in luring him out of this muted silence
where he had sought refuge from the moment he had delivered himself up to the Whites to disclose the topic of the old man who had
appeared before him. This old man didn't live in Pennapolis, but

was from his native country, an elder of his home village, the father of his fathers, the Ancestor ... And that was it. Kadota never again referred to the vision that had ordered him to act.

But, it was a causational leap from that statement to the following excerpt from the police report:

> ... that Kadota (47 years of age) claims to have seen in a
> dream a grimacing mask in the ceiling of his home, an
> old Japanese man who allegedly delivered the order to
> him to kill his entire family and that, consequently,
> to commit such an inexplicable crime, just as in the case
> of other rich Orientals, the gardener, who had money,
> was in all likelihood under the influence of a drug, opium,
> hashish, or other narcotic ...

As I say, this is a stretch, as was the diagnosis of the psychiatrist who concluded there was a seizure-like crisis of *dementia praecox* and who concluded with absolute certainty that this was a case of a deficient and well-determined psychic state. But this does nothing to explain the mechanics of that state of mind.

When I went to visit Kadota in the Junquéry asylum for the criminally insane, the attendant physician warned me that the author of this bloody tragedy had erased everything from his memory and that the insane man conducted himself with utter charm and courtesy. It is true that the Japanese man was calm and had an outwardly friendly demeanour. But what struck me immediately was that his cottage was decorated with representations of fish of every dimension possible that the madman drew wherever he could, using a chunk of coal, even tracing them out on the ground and onto the quilted walls.

"This sketch signifies something," I told the departmental intern who had accompanied me. Everyone knows that in Japan, the fish is the symbol of the race. It seems to me, therefore, that your patient has forgotten nothing and that, on the contrary, he is still under the spell and is still awaiting the sentence of the old man, the order of the ancestor, the Grand Ancestor (*Aieul*), for it was the Ancestor who had forced him to commit his crime. I hold the view that since he had become rich, thus having, in summary, achieved the goal he had set for himself, channeled this Japanese General, who committed seppuku after having placed the flag of the Empire of the Rising Sun on the Port-Arthur fortress, Kadota sacrificed his family on the altar of the genius of his race.

For me, the deed of this virtually invisible settler, who paradoxically had been gentrified and was vainly proud of his Ford—to the degree that it was even a point of pride that he drove himself to the police—was a form of throwing down the gauntlet to the White Man. By carrying out this carnal sacrifice of his own family, I am sure that Kadota thought he was rendering a worthy homage to the courage of his race in the spirit of the descendant of a noble Samurai who commits hara-kiri before the tutelary portrait of the emperor. The key to the crime of Kadota is in the Fish (which is also the symbol of Genitalia or Sex), so it remains an exercise in futility to discern the unfathomable depths of an Oriental, even the most miserable and earthy of peasants.

* * *

The case of Fébronio Indio do Brazil is much more difficult to elucidate, in my opinion, because this sadistic murderer was a Black and a Christian.

Fébronio is a great reader of the Bible. Thus, if he also, as all people of colour, had received the word from the great ancestor of atavism, he could only have received the message directly from God the Father, this jealous god who thunders his wrath on the pages of the Old Testament and whose voice resonates like the roll of a drum in the desert. The voice of God, that masks for this Black a million misleading echoes, colours itself musically, drags him along, troubles his senses, glistens and shimmers since Fébronio was born in Brazil, very far in the interior, in Damantina, Province of Minas Geraes, the ancient province of the gold mines, where all the negroes who come into the world are musicians and singers—the voice of the Father, who spoke to him continuously, echoed in his mind as a familiar refrain, and in an entirely spontaneous manner. Secundo, from the warbling, impossible to define, but bursting out of God only knows what agile and fallacious beast of the Brazilian bush, and a dazzling and quivering deity, knotted and twined, like the Laocoon serpent, to the little Black Jesus and the Blonde Holy Virgin Mary. You can follow the cult and witness the gaudily painted statue, dressed in eagle feathers because this fantastical figure which clasps the Blonde Mother (*"Nossa Senhora de cabellos louros"*) and the Black Christ child (painted flesh-coloured) is a crested being, diaphanous, ocellated like a bird, the contrary of a heavily scaled, dragon-like Tarasque, with egrets and tufts of living bird-of-paradise plumes, and which move and ruffle and flutter in the light of candle flames as if this winged serpent hatched with love, rather than strangled with possession, its divine, mulatto brood. A statue worm-eaten with age is the object of a particular devotion in a Catholic church of Bahia, this superstitious Rome of South American Blacks. Finally, to complete the trinity of confusion, just as his passionate blood brothers whom all music summons into ecstatic dance, deliria and trance-marinated tremens, Fébronio still had to hear *tertio*, a tom-tom voice—returning to him rhythmically, ceaselessly and disturbing like that of an anthropophagic ventriloquist, the insatiable and dissatisfied voice of a grand fetish of Africa, zoomorphic and necrophile—pronounce the master password: TABOO.

* * *

The taboo is the talisman of nagualism, which is the religion of dreams and illusions. Baptism is a blood ceremony, but we are not speaking of blood sprinkled, but blood exchanged, absorbed, integrated, and reincorporated by the initiate who identifies with the great unity through the communion of living blood.

This incorporation is the key to the magic of the Black fetishists who practice incisions, burns, cicatricial scales, skin flakes, the

sharpening of teeth, the deformation of lips or the gibbosity of buttocks, mutilations of the skull or genitalia, the extreme variety of
tattoos, not for reasons of decorative vanity, but for purposes of
sorcery, to identify with the Totem: the tutelary Beast of the clan.

Which clan was Fébronio's, and who was the protector beast
with whom this negro had "become a brother" through the exchange
of blood?

Nobody paid any heed to this line of inquiry—neither the investigating magistrate nor the psychiatrist—to resolve the enigma of
the monster of Rio de Janeiro, the first example of a sadistic serial
killer to appear in Brazil, qualified by one as an "altruistic madman," by another as the "classical profile of a serial killer." But these
two labels are paltry approximations, and I hold the view that until
the Justice system and Science of the White cultures take into
account or study this figured bass that I'm noting in counterpoint—
visions, dreams, voices, random logic and language, key images,
symbolic acts that dominate the story of Fébronio, we will never
understand anything about psychogenesis, the morbid mechanism,
the behavioural aspects of the mentality, or anything of the repressed
subconscious, the imagination, the deliria, the exhaustion of the soul
of the indigenous and the displaced.

When I visited Fébronio inside his prison, I could not possibly
broach these questions of totem and tattoo in one hour because I
know that an initiate would as soon have his tongue ripped out than
respond impromptu to such questions. But, based on certain indicia,
I could reasonably speculate that Fébronio was born into the Buffalo
clan, as are most of the medicine men of Africa who handle iron and
fire and that a young administrator of the circle, making his debuts
in the colony, might mistake as "blacksmiths what" are in fact poi-
soners who quantify the sparks of life and handle elements. Their
hierarchy can be broken down into tutelary demiurges, diviners,
sorcerers, man-leopards or werewolves, walking dead, judges, heal-
ers, exhibitors of larva, spell-casters, trainers of cock-fighters, high
priests, bi-metallic blacksmiths (solar metals, lunar metals), swords-
men, surgeons and butchers.

In my eyes, Fébronio is the distant descendant of a great African sorcerer, as are all the Blacks of Brazil who are deprived by exile from drinking at the live springs of the African mystique and are lost children. In the end, Fébronio is a Métis, notwithstanding his deep skin colour, a Negro-Christian bastard whose intelligence and spirituality have consumed themselves and sunk at the antipodes of the pantheistic tradition and the animist religion of his race.

* * *

Fébronio's father was a butcher.

We know that, from their earliest childhood, he forced his sons to participate in his trade as an executioner of beasts, a "cut-throat" because, in Brazil, the butcher doesn't slaughter; he bleeds. The father initiated the son in the handling of different cutlasses. We also know from this rustic primitive that he was cruel and that for no reason at all, he was happy to crack the whip in his family and that he adored terrorizing his own.

Just as one of his brothers had done, Fébronio ran away from home numerous times. One day, he disappeared for good, abandoning his father's car on a hollowed-out path, the same vehicle the pater familias used during his visits to the hamlets and plantations of the neighbourhood. The ugly, red car of Brazilian butchers from the interior regions due to its dirty-yellow inscription on the side; *Carne Verde*, which means "fresh meat" and not "Carne verte" as one might be inclined to believe, but which is nevertheless more nauseating than the stench that this sinister cart emitted under the noonday sun, that the swarms of sooty, anthrax-carrying flies that escort it or that the carrion eaters, the foul Urubus that survey from their perches or glide over, when emerging from a beaten track, the car stops at the entry of a village comprised of nothing more than bamboo or mud huts.

We find Fébronio again at fourteen years of age, in Rio de Janeiro, where he is jailed by the police for petty theft. He is released, or he escapes. He resumes his life of vagabonding and drifting. He lives from B&Es and petty theft. He is arrested for a new offence. Once again, he is hospitalized because he is homeless. He is detained. And in all the institutions where he sojourns, he is a case of insubordination and exercises a strange power over his unfortunate comrades of misfortune.

The administration classifies him as a hard case. Everyone fears him. Jailers and prisoners alike are convinced this bad seed has the evil eye. It is even whispered that this unregenerate is casting spells and beguiling.

This is the prototype of what, in the black suburbs of Rio, the superstitious people call a "fascinator." One trembles, but people obey such a person, even in a case where the hellion is still learning to ply his trade.

His prestige is immense with his fellow convicts because he is the cruellest and the most intelligent. He re-invents himself as a surgeon, dentist and healer. One day, at the prison infirmary, he steals a scalpel and operates with apparent expertise on a patient being treated for anthrax of the lips. He has the manic obsession of wanting to extract teeth. He treats and he inflicts wounds. It is told that once, inside a Rio police station, where he had been arrested for a theft committed in a bakery, he cut the finger of another detainee to plug up a hole he had punctured with an awl into the belly of a drunkard dozing on a sloping incline. Fébronio claimed he had cured the two wounded.

At seventeen, he is arrested again, this time for fraud, and sentenced to Ile Grande. That is where he begins to read the Bible. Fébronio compares himself to Daniel, who was also young, in exile, and tossed into solitary. And just like his favourite prophet, he begins to proclaim a series of pompous prophecies.

Once he has served his time, Fébronio disappears, and we lose track of him. It is only after several years, at the time of his final arrest—at the time, Fébronio is 32 years of age—that the federal police learn to their stupefaction that during all that time, the monster has never been out of circulation travelling throughout the immense land and that he had opened, naturally without a diploma, a dental office successively in Bahia and Récife in the North, in Belo Horizonte and Barra-do-Pirahy, in the centre, in Curitiba, in Porto Alegre and Pelotas in the south. He even practices medicine—obviously without a diploma—from the Faculty in Santos and in the two capitals of Brazil, Rio and Sao Paulo, where he devises innumerable fraud schemes, suckering dupes and victims in every last one of these cities. Everywhere he passes, he leaves several bodies behind him, boys and adolescents, bearing the same marks of depravity and rape.

What is most extraordinary in this story is that his arrest is not due to the exploits of a vampire but, as we shall see, to the extravagant conduct of a visionary prophet.[7]

* * *

Fébronio returns to Rio, more impoverished and more cunningly sinister than ever.

He is troubled and restless.

He can't figure out why he has returned to the capital, in this grand, rich and beautiful city of Rio de Janeiro, where he has never had any luck.

For some time already, he has been hearing voices. He has always been unstable, but now he begins surrendering to the impulses he could never fully control, but were now in the ascendancy.

He drifts on the Avenida, lingers in public spaces, entrances to movie houses, and tramway terminus stations, where so many coloured stragglers, laggards and dandies park themselves the entire day, waiting for God knows what piece of God-given luck, random

---

7. I would like the biography of Fébronio to be read like a palimpsest, i.e., by attempting to re-establish by way of an intentionally sober and succinct, sparse text that I have just made of his adventures, everything that in the tempestuous career of this monstrous negro that has any resonance or correlation with what we know of the mentality of primitives and the mythology of Africa, everything that transpires, and may be interpreted. This simple summary would take on a singular landscape if we consider that Fébronio's father was a butcher. This signifies that he was a sorcerer by heritage, active or passive, and even if without being conscious of it, his bleeding of animals was a ritual act that he committed. Cracking the whip was a sign of authority, of emancipation or retribution by a former slave, etc.

meeting or stroke of luck to come their way. He mixes in with the crowds of swimmers at Praia Flamengo, Praia Vermelha, de Copacabana or Ipanéma, this series of fine-sanded, half-crescent beaches that stretch out as far as the Praia do Arpoador.[8] He then walks from Leblon to the Gavéa, not attempting to disguise or hide himself. He as if the police didn't exist or as if he had never had any run-ins with them, under the compulsion of a dreadful obsession, a rising impulsion of power and domination as he felt that the time was drawing nigh for him to reveal himself to the world.

When he roams the streets—that all lead to the sea—and when he ambulates amidst the cries of joy of the horns and the din of trams—when he lays down on the beach, he receives the ambient, throaty laughs of the prestigious white women roaming freely, the care-free carioca *mûlatresses*, the slews of happy toddlers and children. The clusters of joyful bairns resemble cherubs whose mothers dip into the waves and then rise to the skies like an offering. Fébronio closes his eyes, seized by a vertigo that is not only due to his hollow stomach but especially to the intoxication triggered by the luxury of the capital, the noise of the streets, the lyrics of the passers-by, the murmur of the waves, the shouts of toddlers playing, the raw seductive voices of the women, the sun penetrating his face, the heat seeping into his pores, the scalding, numbing sand, all of this combines to trigger a composite emotion ... it is as if this delusional negro has to drink in the entire ocean and then be hurtled into space, where he hovers for a long time, exhilarated by this vocational summons that levitates him into the air and suspends him in the skies as if the murmurings of the great city is a homage, a smoking pyre of incense rising towards him, meant for him.

When he opens his eyes, he feels the sensation of falling from a great height, the impression of returning from afar.

The space, the immensity, the palpitating light, the raw skies, the dazzling sea of the Bay of Guanabara, and the steamrolling waves of the Atlantic have his temples throbbing. Finally, his gaze

---

8. Harpooners Beach

settles on the Sugar Loaf, this granite cone that, from the depths of the ocean, in a single spray, shoots azure from its depths, like a dream of stone emerging from a fringe of foam and from a hemline of palm trees. Like a throne ... a stone table ... a sacrificial altar, erected in full view of Brazil's capital, like a locus specially chosen by the fates. Delectable and inevitable.

So, Fébronio arises and departs, turning his back on the magnificent bay, erring in the streets, losing himself inside the city, straying from the beaten path. Yet, his steps always, and ineluctably, at random times of day and night, draw him back to the sea, where he can admire the spiked peak that exercises a magnetic pull upon him, while filling him with a distinct fear as if the location bears his mark.

Fébronio doesn't sleep during the night because he fears the dreams that visit him. "When you are strong, you engage in combat with sleep," he tells himself. "You cannot be the prey of the shadow world." And he takes a vow that he will never sleep again. So, during the night, he will not lie down.

He continues his perambulating in and out of Rio's interminable streets, wandering onto deserted strands, roaming like a damned soul in the Rio suburbs stretching out beneath him, between the hills concealing forbidden villages, and far, far behind the mountains, enveloped in small and large brush & flora, where an entire floating population celebrates on fixed dates, certain Fridays, mysterious ceremonies such as the *macumba* or the *condomblé*, savage ritual sacrifices, spirit offerings and dances from the depths of innumerable cloistered neighbourhoods that penetrate like a wound into the heart of this magnificent but enigmatic modern capital of more than two million inhabitants.

And when the vagabond, the famished, the famished, off-centre vagabond passes like a shadow in the streets, his silhouette sliding over the façade of homes bleached by the moon, retreating into the darkness, chased by dogs. This cursed soul digs his hands into his pockets, and caresses lovingly his dentist's forceps, his small surgeon's kit that he can no longer separate himself from, a large penknife, a mandatory weapon for any drifter, and the fine and long needles and flask of indelible ink that formed his equipment of a tattoo artist.

"I have a mission. I am the Prince of Fire!" Fébronio murmurs. And this miserable man feels a mad rush of pride possessing his entire being.

* * *

One dawn morning, Fébronio finds himself at the summit of the Sugar Loaf. Having started from the concealed small beach of the Urca, he climbs through the thicket and coppice, the rocky debris, the prickly pears that form a virtually impregnable bastion at the foot of the majestic cone, having assaulted the colossus by its rock face that looks out over the ocean and that is reputed to be utterly inaccessible. He ascends gradually, gripping the uneven asperities with his fingernails, risking dozens, maybe a hundred times, falling into the ocean. It takes him the entire night to reach the summit on his hands and feet.

At that early hour, nobody is in sight on the wooden terrace of the Belvedere viewpoint. The restaurant is closed, and the first funicular railway has yet to arrive. Fébronio inspects the premises, briefly considers breaking into the pavilion, and then falls under the charm of the marvellous city's panorama that stretches before him.

As God, he dominates "his" capital, and he has the impression that he can destroy his "mistress city" and redeem it according to his will.

The cock crows.

Fébronio is drawn out of his contemplation by a shutter that bangs against the façade of the restaurant chalet and by the spinning and whining of the cable car's wheel, which has just kicked into gear.

He leaps back, jumps over the balustrade, allows himself to slide into the scree-strewed slope and arrives instantly, one hundred metres lower, on the dome in the form of a dromedary or, better, the back of an elephant serving as the last buttress before the vertiginous protrusion, the polished mass of the pyramid of the Sugar Loaf which rises up and then drops off in a dizzy spin into the entrance of the Guanagara, this bay that is unique in the world.

The location is overgrown with old bush. Fébronio uses his knife to clear a path through the branches, vines, and cactus. Finally, he manages to pierce up until a space of small clearing that looks like a skylight over Rio.

From this asylum perched on the cliff, the silence and solitude are as complete as if Fébronio has lost himself a hundred thousand leagues into the interior of the lands of his immense motherland, which is still three-quarters virgin territory.

The morning drags on.

Niched like a vulture on his apron perch, the madman contemplates "his" city crushed under the heat. Intermittently, he blinks his eyes, and his eyelid closes itself, the image of his prey internalized, embedded onto his radar.

A hundred million cicadas buzz and click incessantly from the floor of the enormous solar dome over which Fébronio presides, like the Magi King coming from the Indies on the back of an elephant. He feels the vibrations of the electrical plant beneath, the dynamo … and when the cable-car passes, a hundred metres up in the air, Fébronio knots two blades of grass into a cross, performing the cabalistic ring with the thumb and the ring finger of the left hand, the index and the baby finger as horns, the median finger folded forward, and he spits out. "Let this cursed string break and unravel! Death, o misery of my mother!" he recites aloud. He throws himself to the ground and rhythmically knocks his head against the soil as he utters this imprecation.

For a long time, he remains prone, first on his belly, then on the back, to not lose the cable car from view. He has ascended to a fierce state of exaltation, his eyes wide open, all his strength and will focus on carrying out his cursed mission by severing this damned cable and triggering the fall of the gondola, which, like a filthy fly, would soil the sky and the azure.

The negro sorcerer trembles in excited anticipation.

And then, suddenly, he has a vision.

Has he fallen asleep?

Fébronio categorically denies it. Not that time, he says. And it is only later, when he returns several times to the same location and submits to the curses and hexes of the Devil, that he sleeps. Perhaps Satan has waited for him to fall asleep to possess him and beat him with blows. But he swears that he never slept when "the young Blonde Lady" appeared before him, especially not when "*A Moàa de cabellos louros*" appeared before him for the first time.

It must have been around noon.

Fébronio is lying on his back, immobile, holding his breath.

He relates that his eyes had left their orbit like a pair of red rats escaped from the gates of hell to gnaw the cursed cable of the lift attaching to the earth to the heavens like a dead weight. He has slept so little that he recalls perfectly having felt a snake come to slither around him and then wrap itself around his head. And then the cold of the serpent penetrated within and began to freeze up his marrow, and he allowed himself to channel its full horror. Suddenly, the space burst like a large shattering glass. There appeared before him "a Lady," he writes later in the book that was destroyed by the police, "*a Blonde Lady, with long golden hair, who declared to me that God was not dead and that I had been given the mission to announce him to the entire world. I had the mission to write a book and mark the young elected with the letters D.C.V.X.V.I., a tattoo that is the symbol of the Living God, and irrespective of the deployment of violence!*"

* * *

Without a family, homeless, friendless, shattered, weary, exhausted by the life he has been leading since his return to the capital, dying of hunger and thirst, more abandoned and poorer than Job, the mind derailed by the vision that had just shattered his spirit, his compass thoroughly skewed, Fébronio wonders how he can fulfil this mission that he has been charged with and that he has accepted with enthusiasm. But now he doubts his strength and faculties, shifting sequentially through sadness to maudlin chagrin to illumination, flickering joy to delirium. Throughout this undulating house of mirrors, he is juggling his knife, admiring his tattoo artist's equipment, his kit, his rusted forceps, that he holds up like a chalice before him in the bush and that shine in the sunlight. Then he falls to his knees in supplication, emerging to calculate his more sinister and cleverer chances than ever. Meditative, hesitant, and triumphant, Fébronio remains closed off in the tangled bushes at the edges of the Sugar Loaf for several days.

"There," he testifies before the investigating magistrate who wants to know the detailed use of his time, there is "no mato dentro."

> "Of course, I was deep in the forest. I was inanimate, near dead, after the visit of the Blonde Lady. Then, despondent to find myself without money, homeless, and an orphan after the revelation of my destiny, it is natural that I felt the need to penetrate the furthest possible into the *maquis* backcountry, where I hid myself to relax and rest my body. Just like a philosopher from the days of Antiquity, I spent thus three or four days, far from the world, lost in high cogitations and working out the basis for my prophetic book: *The Revelations of the Prince of Fire,* a book that I brought to the printer and that appeared in the bookstores less than three months later."

I could never procure this gospel of Fébronio, notwithstanding promises to set aside a copy for me. I am left with no other conclusion then that for the last ten years, my Brazilian friends—members of parliament, physicians, lawyers, journalists, writers—were no more fortunate than me in their investigations and searches in bookshops and stalls. We know now that the federal police destroyed this book right down to its last copy, and according to the statements of his editor, the end result was a volume of 67 numbered pages, published in Rio in 1925. On the first page appears the following verse of Fébronio:

Eis aqui, meu Santo
Tabernaculo-Vivente
hoje dedicado a vos
os encantos que ligaste
hontem a mim na Fortaleza
do meu Fiel Diadema Excelso[9]

Page 2 bears the dedication to:

"Altissimo Deus-Vivo"
(To the celestial Living God)

No information is available on how Fébronio could have obtained the money to print his little book because a vanity press printed this publication.

Interrogated by the police, his editor explained:

> One day, a negro entered my shop carrying a rolled manuscript wrapped inside the newspaper. It was illegible, written in ink and pencil on various scraps of paper, many of which were P.T.T. telegram forms.
>
> Having informed him that I couldn't accept a manuscript presented in such poor condition, the man returned several days later with a type-set manuscript. The printing of his wild imaginings was delayed further because the negro was penniless. He thus returned to see me on several occasions, each time making instalments until he had paid 800 milreis (approx. 2000 francs) corresponding to the publication price. After that, he often returned to my shop, at various times, bringing copies of his brochures that he paid for in cash and carried in small packages.

---

9. It is here, my Venerated one!/ Living Tabernacle/ that I today dedicate to you/ the incantations with which you have enchanted me/ here in my prison/ O Preexcellent (Diademe) of my Faith! [Note: B.C. Translation in turn translated by D.M.]

One day, I told him I had attempted to read his book but couldn't make head or tail of it. And this is precisely how he responded to my remark: 'I confess that all that is muddled, but you will better understand when we see, here in this capital, when you witness the Living God walking naked upon the Avenida.'

I realize today that this negro who had not wished to sign his work is the negro that you have just described to me: the infamous Fébronio.

When the magistrate asked why his brochure did not bear the author's name, the magus became indignant and responded: "I didn't sign my book because the Son of Light has no ambition for celebrity. It is sufficient to reveal to mankind the mission of the Prince of Fire."

Fébronio's Book[10]

Here are several rare excerpts from this lost manuscript: I cut out these quotes from a local newspaper. They all deal with the mission Fébronio claimed had been visited upon him.

Page 10: "… and this was a supreme act of his charity when the Living Tabernacle of the Orient chose from among the living ones, on an island, the living child, the heir of a living trumpet announcing to the world, chiming day and night, the existence of his eternal companion, come from the Rising Sun …"

Page 16: "… and this was a loyal act of his perfect love when the Holy Living Tabernacle ordered the crowning of the young living child in the Orient …"

---

10. A page from Fébronio's book, *As Revelaçoes do principe do fogo*, discovered by Carlos Augusto Calil in 1997. The handwritten notations are probably those of the poet Mario de Andrade.

Page 28: "... and He came to designate among men the unhappiest, the insignificant young man, but one of such precious value, the living-son of the Magi of antiquity, as He wished to incarnate and have this celebrated by you in his Church, as He had taught to you how to prophesize and announce the Life by the voice of Death ..."

The carioca journalist to whom we are indebted for these three texts, which are the only three known fragments of the Gospel according to Fébronio, adds a commentary, which is a typical example of this manner of separating truth and deceit that is proper to a columnist of a small local paper addressing his subscribers:

The prophecies of Fébronio Indio do Brazil constitute a unique document that allows us to follow to the end the riskiest and most adventurous cavalcades of the derailed imagination of this madman. But this document is also a testimony of the ignorance and the lack of culture of this Black. At most, we can detect the traces of a profound influence from the Bible, which Fébronio had obsessively read from inside the prison walls. That was where he turned for legitimacy, comparing himself to the prophet Daniel, and this delirious negro interpreted his dreams, and these dreams became the motives for his criminal rampages.

* * *

From his deliria, his dreams, his nightmares, and his visionary illusions, Fébronio related a detailed account to the psychiatrist to whom he had been assigned for observation before directing the attention of the jury towards the inner workings of this man-leopard during his trial before the Assizes Court and during which time the proceedings were ordered to be in camera.[11]

---

11. The Brazilian Code doesn't recognize the death penalty. The maximum sentence is thirty years imprisonment for first degree murder. Fébronio was incarcerated in the Manicomio Judiciario of Rio de Janeiro (1927) where this sadistic Black is still imprisoned (1937) [B.C.]

First dream: "The Blonde Lady had barely disappeared," he informed his physician, "when I fell into a deep sleep and through the intermediary of a vision, I became aware that not all of the spirits were in favour of my mission and that because of that, I would be locked in mortal combat with the ill winds unleashed by the demons ...

Second dream: "Only a few days had passed—I was still hidden in the high maquis, between the Sugar Loaf and the barracks of the marine commandos whose bugle sounds reached up towards my solitude—I fell once again into a deep sleep, and I saw in my dreams a Master Bird resembling a dragon, who told me that the Prince of Shadows was not pleased at all with the mission assigned to me by the Blonde Lady. This bird was a terrifying beast, with a very long beak, the tiny voice of a child, and vermilion feathers, the colour of fire. Firstly, this beast attempted to tempt me by seduction. She directed a thousand graces and a thousand charms my way and conjured up before my eyes platters of culinary delights, a myriad of victuals. Then, she offered me enormous amounts of money and promised me glory so long as I agreed to give up this mission that I had accepted and provided I did not write my book.

"Then, faced with my solemn refusal, the dragon bristled and uttered horrible threats, telling me that he had already killed Christ and John the Baptist and that I didn't frighten him. And the bird-genie moved away, screeching that he would kill me and devour me, break my bones with his wide wings, stomp upon me, leaving me bruised and bloodied. I was in such pain being crushed under his belly that I cried out as he flew away: 'If you want to kill me, kill me now and devour me!' And then, I left the woodland and wandered for a long time in the city, hunched over, utterly worn out, filled with a great sadness that wouldn't allow me to think or to write. Without knowing why, I was full of doubts about the effectiveness of my mission and convinced of my weakness and my powerlessness to fight with the devil."

Second appearance of the Blonde Lady: Eight or fifteen days later, having returned to the forest at the same spot, the same Blonde Lady made another apparition:

"She didn't look happy," Fébronio said. And, calling me by my name: 'Fébronio,' she said, 'Why are you not writing, and why aren't you doing anything?' Then she ordered me to find a sword to fight the dragon that was terrifying me. But, first, before being invincible in this singular combat, I had to, in her words, select ten young boys, tattoo them, and mark them with symbolic letters.

"Before leaving and with a deep expression of sadness, my Lady said again: 'Fébronio, if you doubt in yourself and do not believe in the virtue of your mission, the dragon will emerge victorious in your duel with him and the Bird shall continue to dominate the world, to darken the daylight and to cause the shedding of tears.'"[12]

Between the second visitation of the Blonde Lady and the third dream of Fébronio that can be situated, the series of ritual crimes and the publication of the *Revelations of the Prince of Fire* triggered the arrest of the madman by a police sergeant.

Fébronio directs the focus of his voracious tracking inside the city. He chooses his pathetic victims preferably from the ranks of the simpletons, the poor, seducing young hawkers and peddlers, newspaper criers, shoe-shine boys or these poor boys using whitening to decorate the tires of luxury cars and parked taxis with Tenerife motifs and arabesques, unemployed boy runners, street performers, a ship-boy, a young recruit, urchins and vagabonds. He offers them presents, sweet words, work, tempting promises, and even money, leading them to believe he is the sole heir to an immensely rich old aunt. He charms them with turns of phrase, preaches his new religion of the Living God, recites excerpts from his manuscript and later reads passages from his printed book. And, the innocents, who have come to believe they were among the elect, take the fatal step of accompanying him where he wishes and fatally, up to his hide-out

---

12. See in my Negro Anthology, chap. IV: The Guinnés animals, the rain bird, p. 39 [Note of B.C.]

on Sugar Loaf, where he would initiate them by tattooing them before slitting their throats or eviscerating them.

"I was master of them all," declares Fébronio with pride. "But immediately after a sacrifice, I would be powerless to stop myself from falling into a heavy sleep and even when I defended myself with my faithful sword, I remained a victim of the Devil who beat me with blows and half-strangled me and, upon awakening, I would have no choice but to begin anew."

Third dream of Fébronio: "Since I took up the practice of tattooing young boys to redeem them; in my dreams, I found myself fighting the dragon. This time, the fabulous bird transformed into a steer that, upon seeing me, charged upon me, booming out a shout that caused earth and heaven alike to tremble: 'I am Satan, Satan in person, and you have been irritating me for a long time, Fébronio. I am going to gore you ... I have to tell you, doctor, that bulls know me and this big *caracul*[13] made no more impression upon me, no more than those whom I'd seen slaughtered in my father's shop. He could go ahead and grimace and holler in a stertorous booming bass that he was Satan, Satan in person. I wasn't afraid because I knew where to touch a bull, and his bellowing rage wouldn't distract me from bleeding him cleanly, as I saw it done by my father. There is a stroke so simple that a child could cut their carotid artery when these furious beasts put their head down and charge at you. With the slightest bit of sang-froid, you can stab them between the shoulders, which causes them to fall to their knees and force a torrent of blood out of the nostrils. So, I ran to back myself up against a tree trunk and waited to confront the monster head-on. I was very calm, and this bull, who wanted to gorge me, made me smile.

"I was naked, as always, since I began celebrating my sacrifices in my clearing, and I had my naked sword in my hand. It was around noon. The sun shone harshly onto the Sugar Loaf, and a circle of vultures flew above without casting a shadow, which was a

---

13. Caracul: race of indigenous bulls. [Note of B.C.]

fortunate omen. This time I held the Devil! But then a miracle occurred. Each time the bull attacked me, the tree I leaned against grew and lifted me into the air. Each time the Cursed One distanced himself to make a U-turn, the tree shrank and set me down on the ground so that my thrusts of the sword and the furious plunge of the bull's horns clashed together in the void. It seemed to last an eternity. And the bull foamed with rage, and I cried out in anger against this treachery because I knew I had to conquer. I performed flourishing moulinets with my sword to pull myself out of God knows what powerful magic when I felt myself held from behind, and a police sergeant had handcuffed me.

"Death and damnation! This idiotic sergeant had gathered up my sword, and as I shouted a warning that the bull was charging us down, this imbecile began laughing and hit me over the head. Then I saw the bull jump into the air and fly upwards, darkening the sky, the bay, and the sea, and a large roaring cloud descended upon the great city I wished to redeem. And everything went dark. When I emerged from my dream, I was at the police station, and everyone was pulling and pushing me, questioning me day and night without any relief: 'What were you doing in the woods, dirty nigger? Why were you naked? What's with this tattoo that you have on the chest? And why this sword? And what did you do with the children, Fébronio, filthy bottom-feeding scavenger? Cough it up! And why this? And why that?' And they beat me. As for me, I denied everything and kept my mouth shut because my book wasn't written for them. And today, I'm asking you, doctor, why, but why has my Blonde Lady not returned, and I haven't seen her a third time? I'm telling you, you, you are all the henchmen of the Devil.

* * *

In the opinion of the guards, I was lucky to have visited on a good day. I had already been conversing with him for an hour, and never had the monster of the Rio penitentiary been so calm nor testified with such confidence to anyone.

His fire was extinguished. The shadows enveloped the grand cage. I saw Fébronio shiver. The stench of the prison had me gagging. It was time to leave. Besides, the longer it went on, the more this tête-à-tête with this Black bothered me because I couldn't do anything for him.

But before leaving him, I asked Fébronio again: "And when you were high up there, alone walking in the old scrub of the Sugar Loaf, what was your favourite part of the day? I find it difficult to believe you were always *tristinho* and in a funk. You had moments of joy, no?"

"My favourite hour? O, my French colleague, you don't know it? Come on. The marvel of Rio is the evening when night falls and all the lights of the capital light up at once in a single stroke. The hundred thousand street lamps of Rio! You don't have that in Paris, do you?"

It should be pointed out that, although Paris is the City of Light, two capitals of the Austral hemisphere are richer in lights than Paris, jealously disputing with each other the right to this title as record-holder of electrical extravagance.

I refer to Sydney in Australia and Rio de Janeiro in South America.

As soon as news arrives that Sydney city council has voted a new credit to amplify the lighting already flooding the queen of the South Seas, the prefect of Rio de Janeiro doubles his outlay to multiply the nocturnal feast of fairies that twinkles invitingly over his sleeping city like a bride in the most grandiose landscape of the world—kilometre upon kilometre of new roads and ramps. Thousands and thousands of new power lines are added to the fresco of the Bay of Guanabara, the beaches, the islands, to all these scintillating lines that converge and intertwine the bay, like a coil of luminous pearls around the neck of an Indian deity, around the sombre, majestic rock peak of the Sugar Loaf.

But notwithstanding the display of a feast and this fairy-like illumination, and this modern improvisation unceasingly renewed, notwithstanding these ceaseless rebirths of tropical constellations, I cannot watch this rock from the bow of a passenger ship tacking seaward to take me back to France without shuddering at the recollection of the forty or sixty skeletons that were found, not buried in the depths of the castle of Bluebeard, but exposed in the noonday sun, under the watchful eye of vultures, among the cactus, the palm trees, the mimosas, the ancient shrub and bramble that haunted Fébronio, and many of whom were never identified.

TAKE THIS CUP OF BLOOD

Part I—Black Rain

Champagne 1915

THE DAY AFTER the catastrophic failure of the "great offensive."[1]

Forty-eight hours after my amputation, another attack was in the offing in the sector.

The Supply Corps needed my bed and my bloodied shirt. I found myself naked on a stretcher in the wireworks where they had severed my arm, waiting for the arrival of a convoy of Ford ambulances on their way to evacuate us. Hundreds of wounded—a chorus of undulating pain—chanted from the four cardinal points of a vast factory floor, a scattered labyrinth of machine parts and dismounted boilers and dismembered men—surgery station 55 in the rear.

The sky was black. Unrelenting rain. Dirty weather.

It was around nine or ten in the evening—the 1st or 2nd day of October.

---

1. The brainchild of General Joffre, launched on 25 September 1915, the "Great Offensive of Champagne" was a particularly costly battle. Cendrars was wounded on the 4th day, the 28th, by a German machine gunner: "In approximately three hours of combat, the regiment lost 608 legionnaires out of 1960 and 29 officers our of 431 (Jean Bastier, "Blaise Cendrars legionnaire (1914–1915)", in *Cendrars et la guerre*, Armand Colin, 1995, p. 50.

The shelling and the gunfire from the front increased in cadence and volume. Behind me, a 75 fired at point-blank range on enemy planes. The buzz of aircraft racing low over the factory roofs terrified us even more than the heavy artillery explosions which, on the left and the right, pummelled the remains of the Somme-Py ruins.

Men stopped in their tracks, crouching or diving in terror to the ground. Men straddling my stretcher, splattering mud onto me. Men zig-zagging blindly between heaps of twisted metal. Men crumbling, collapsing, and burying the unlucky ones with their own bodies as they expired. Everywhere men, *capiche*? Men! Scattering, screaming, howling, wailing, groaning. My amputated arm now caused me such pain that my teeth had sunk into my tongue, biting to keep from unleashing a raging cry from the depths of the cauldron. In fits and starts, long shakes reverberated through my body. Hypothermic shaking worsened by the sweeping rain. I am prone on my narrow stretcher, nude, immobilized, and now numbed, unable to command my body to move and paralyzed like the mother of a newborn by the enormous bandage, my stump, the Christ-child[2] in swaddling clothes. I am a man, or what is left of a man, clinging to my flank, this strange, grafted life-form. I couldn't so much as twitch without triggering a universe of pain. I was unable to caress my remaining limb with this bulky swab, the original white now saturated with the river of crimson it had soaked up. I felt an atrocious burning and realized that my lifeblood was in a fugue, escaping the veins that had held it safe only hours previous. It was leaving me, drop by drop, and I was helpless to stem the tide. Because you can't stop the heart. But my heart, with every regular beat, unleashed another wave of blood that I could feel, as if I had seen it spurt out of the end of my severed hand. These pulsations, morally and physically unbearable, allowed me to count time to keep just this side of sane.

---

2. In this captivating comparison of the amputee to a newborn, and the stump as a babe-in-arms, is the sketch of a major theme for the left-handed writer, of rebirth through the wound.

The exact time that, within the furious fray of this horrible night, of which I have recorded every last detail, flowed out inexorably, each second, every fraction of a second, containing an eternity.

Two or three hours went by like this.

Between two air raids, between two stampedes, between the sequences of the 75-mm field gun firing wildly and recoiling, between the collapse of the neighbourhood buildings, the porters, nurses, the old Territorials, bustling and tending to the worst wounded cases, who at any cost had to be evacuated, distributed evacuation cards, like porters after a press run in a train station stick labels to packages. And that's why a sergeant who had gone mad and was stricken with fear stuck a dog tag on my ankle, my amputee ID, without so much as a word or even a look at the naked man turning blue from the cold under the rain. And the most droll is that this sergeant got it right.

As I would find out later that day, it was my dog tag that he had stuck onto me.

The vans came after midnight. They arrived in the yard, still hitting the gas, loaded up in haste. They took off in reverse, u-turned on two wheels in front of the portal, and raced into a night bursting with shells, weaving and dodging between demolished houses to re-join the road and the smashed-up remains leading towards the rear.

The ambulances entered two, three at a time. The convoy had been bombed on the way in, and the drivers were frantic to leave, fearing they would get caught in a barrage of fire on their return since, to hear their words, they wanted to get the hell out and arrive at Somme-Py before a convoy of munitions that they had passed en route. They didn't want to get caught in the barrage of gunfire that this reinforcement of munitions was sure to unleash on the cursed village. All the news was alarming. While lending a hand to the team of porters, the drivers shoved the patients of Surgery Station 55 into their cars. Most would have been classified as unfit to transport in ordinary times.

Finally, one of these little Fords stopped in front of me. A poor beggar placed to my right was first on. Then another. A third, they had retrieved from God knows where, and then it was my turn. But the driver, a large slab of bearded meat, barged in, "*Ah, non!* Now, I've seen everything! I'm going to get a sheet ..." The good man disappeared and reappeared with a rag that he tossed onto me, saying: "There you go, my friend. Now, let's get out of here. It is disgusting, but it'll warm you up ..." And they loaded me aboard, fourth in the van, forcing me to slide my head forward as if into the jaws of an oven, then sealed the tarp down over me. The ambulance lurched forward in a fit and a start. This triggered shouts of pain from the four poor bastards covered in blood, bandaged and ravaged, one of whom was me.

* * *

I recall that the man lying prone beneath me, to my left, started the symphony ...

The Ford hurtled ahead, skidding through the road riddled with shell holes.

The van transporting us pitched, reeled, swayed, swerved, yawed like a Medusa raft, skidded onto the lower shoulder, and leap-frogged over piles of stones. I jolted, trundled, ricocheted, and thunked from one crater hole to the next. I was playing a pin-and-ring game with the devil when the motor's furious whirr heightened the madness.

I was a hysterical madman cramped up on his mattress or a fakir mystic in a trance whose discombobulated spirit flees into the beyond and whose stigmatized remains, abandoned on his bed arches, begin to gravitate. I braced myself on my stretcher, which allowed me to move out of my body and hover over myself. This was amidst the jolts and bumps and the tremors that launched me into another beyond of relentless pain. I was no longer human. I had plunged into the depths of my wound, like sinking into a narcotic. My spirit had dropped off a cliff and fell into the abyss.

—Oh! Aie! ... we groaned. Sometimes, a single cry would pierce through. That prolonged screech of pain tore us asunder. I am ashamed to say who of the four of us unless it were me, had howled out this hollow, terrified cry while the ambulance forged forward as best he could.

—Maman! ... maman! ... bawled the man prostate above me. O maman! ...

This four-penny opera rang incessantly inside this infernal beater of an improvised ambulance and held centre stage until the vehicle finally stopped at Châlons-sur-Marne.

—Maman, maman! ... rattled the man above me. O maman! ...

—*Halt Schurred, Sauhund!*[3] Came the insult from the lower bunk. While the wounded legionnaire lisped: *"Ti peux pas te tai'e, hé? La madame ta mamanye est pas si bête, y est pas allé veni'pou'toivoi'ici. Ti y est pas 'aisonnable di tut, petit, pas pou'un petit sou! Moi, le toubib y m'a avoi'coupé les deux jambes et moi ya pas avoi'guielé pou'ça! Ti peux pas la bucler, hé, disdonc, mosieû. Toi, y a beaucoup ballot ...*[4]

The wounded legionnaire in the upper bunk was bawling in an increasingly shrill, cacophonic screech, a throat-splitting clamour, stretching out crescendo and decrescendo. The German next to me insulted him, anything to shut him up. The negro, who in an instant yielded to fury, suddenly started to kick up a racket upwards, striking the tarp and bellowing:

—*Chauffeu', chauffeu'! A'été, a'été! Y a qu'à descend'e, moi. Y a un sale Boche là-dedans. Vive la France! ...*[5]

I felt my fever like a depth charge. I was losing consciousness. From the horror, from the suffering, the vertigo, from pure extenuation —when *presto*, the car stopped, and a woman's gentle voice spoke to us from outside:

—Give me your dog tags quickly, my children. You've struck it lucky. There's a nice train here leaving for Biarritz. Quick now, get going! ...

---

3. Shut your face, asshole!
4. Can't you just close your beak, hé? La madame, your mama, she ain't so dumb, she ain't comin' here, and she can't hear you crying. You ain't reasonable, not one centime worth of sense In yo' head, you feeble & flimsy. Me, the bones, he saw off my two legs, you don't hear me whining about dat! Can't you just sew those two lips together, you nitwit!
5. Dwiva, Dwiwa! Stop, stop! Toss me out, me! Is a foul Kwout in there. *Vive la France!"*

We were in a Châlons borough. As they were removing the tarp and hands were groping, fiddling, fingering us, inspecting our evacuation cards, stamping them, granting visas, and recording them, I spotted an arm handing me a bottle of cognac, and I heard another voice—the voice of a woman—saying: "Here, drink. This will do you good, little one!" ...

I grabbed the bottle greedily. The car was already departing. "Bon voyage! Bon voyage!" clamoured the voices. I emptied the bottle in a single draught ... and fell into darkness.

* * *

By the time I regained consciousness, my stretcher had been stored in a railway yard. I detected the reflection of a blue light mirrored in puddles close by. The clock marked 3 am. The sputter of a locomotive choking up smoke. Then, the interminable dreariness of an endless train screeching against rails. I figured it couldn't be long before someone would come and pick me up. Prone on the asphalt, partly concealed under the car's chassis, I was out of the rain and, for now, not worried about my fate. The motor was idling, flushing its hot exhaust into my face, and the stern face of this scrapyard was somehow keeping me going. Only my severed arm was causing me pain.

The train that had arrived at the station was now departing. Rain, black rain ... the gutters overflowing. The motor fell silent ... and I plunged again into sleep or unconsciousness, driven there by the searing pain. It was the ambulance driver, who left to his own devices, had to load me into his car and manage the stretcher as best as he could, i.e., by crushing the arm and tossing me casually on board.

On top of that, the man was unconscious. "*Oh, là là!* The bastards, the useless fucking layabouts! Not a single bastard ready to cover my back," he griped. "Just trying to get close to the fire. I wouldn't mind doing a bit of tourism ... Then he added, spotting me watching him: "Don't tell me that it's nothing but laughs to go at this time for a stroll in town. Well, *mon pote*, you think this is a joy ride! Come to think of it, you were singing a fucking ditty on the road getting out here. No. *j'en ai ma claque, tu sais. Elle n'est rien moche*[6], their fucking war. That's it for me. I'm out. If it goes on much longer, I'm deserting ..."

Then he settled down: "So, I hurt you, did I, old man? Please don't hold it against me. These goddam porters, I've fucking had it with them. We're supposed to be shoulder-to-shoulder. They won't lift a finger, the sons-of-bitches. I've already done two trips since last night. The Krauts hit us hard. What do you think? Having to drag poor bastards like you through all this shit, what do you expect? It drives me mad. My skin's turning inside-out. Me, I'm a mechanic, not a goddam butcher. I'm not trained for this. You think there's not enough going on here to give a man jaundice to see all these train station snipers waltzing with these Dames de France and their twit of a major! And the pompous brass hat, let's talk about that, *mon colon*! Talk about a goddam zealot. Bastard. When I hear him saying the mangled boys sent to him are worthless, I'm tempted to drive a bayonet right up his arse. He pulled that act with you. He didn't want to let you on the train in Biarritz. He said that you were feverish and drunk, and he forced you into a U-turn."

"So, where are you bringing me?" I asked the driver, who was re-firing up his motor for departure.

"I'm taking you to Sainte-Croix, the *évêché*, the bishopric; it's a good hospital. And then, it's close to my garage."

"I'm wiped out, you get that? And I know somebody who's going to pay for this."

"How far is it from here?"

"Don't worry about it. A quarter of an hour, if that. You'll be able to sleep there. A nice hostel. Sainte-Croix is rich. Exotic pussy in numbers, and nothing wrong with the grub. Suffering Mary, you are lucky to run into me. I know this toilet bowl like the back of my hand. I'm telling you, it's a perfect pit stop, and you can believe me

---

6. I'm fed up to the back teeth. Tell you what, it's nasty and it's rotten and foul, this war of theirs.

on that one. Anybody else would have brought you to the military hospital. But the priests take good care of you. Don't worry about that. You're there, man."

"And the others? The others aren't coming? I'm all alone, then?"

"*Mince alors*, you're a curious one. What's your problem? You must know everything? And what were you in civilian life, *imbecile*, to be such a busybody with others? No, you're a moron, that's what you are. You want a cigarette?"

So, he stuck a smoke into my craw. And, maybe the black dog was chewing him to the bone, but as he placed me, he kept talking. "All right, since you must know everything, here you go. That loud-mouthed piece of Senegalese shit, and that fucking kraut, they're on the train, and they couldn't give a shit about you, all right, so right now, they're on their way to Biarritz. As for that runt who was squealing like a pig and getting under our skin, bawling away, *maman, maman*! He checked out. Dust-to-dust, pal. Did you miss that? When they tried to unload him at the station, he was spewing rivers of blood out of his mouth. Fucking geyser he was. Bon Dieu, you're covered in his blood. And you didn't even notice? And my bedsheet is no good anymore, and now I've got to pinch another one. Oh-la-la, what a job, it's, fucking endless, no goddam end to it."

On that note, the driver turned his back to me, triggered a cacophony of grinding gears, and sped off into the tortuous alleyways of Châlons, accelerating into the curves as if he were slashing and mowing down a cursed harvest during his round of the old city.

Part II: The Bishopric

I don't know how long this cursed Red Cross truck took to bring me to the bishopric, and I don't know how this mad dash ended. From what I heard later, I died and returned to life a dozen times at least. But, when I returned a final time to life, I once again found myself naked on my stretcher, except this time the stretcher was in the middle of a gigantic hall festooned in decorative ancient wood panelling.

A majestic oak stairwell, which was giving me vertigo, climbed, ascended four, five, six levels from the polished floor where I lay prone, back to the roof, lost somewhere in the heights, in the darkness, nothing but the beams and joists sentries to my oppression.

Not a sound. Not even a crack. I was stunned. The silence was absolute.

The pompous architecture, the grandeur, the austerity, the nobility, the proportionality, the dimensions of this monumental stairwell, the coats-of-arms on the panels, the calm, and the peace came from another age, another century, another era. Everything seemed an enemy to me, implacable. A hollow terror now seeped into me, as it were, a terror of being forgotten in this macabre décor. I couldn't tear my gaze away from the sole and unique bulb still illuminating the magnificent chandelier that lit the sombre, immense stairwell cage from top to bottom. I couldn't tear my gaze away because I knew I would fall into the vortex from one second to the next.

I was tossing and turning on my stretcher, gesticulating, and not only with my remaining left hand, which I still couldn't figure out how to use, but also brandishing this right hand, this hand that I had just lost, that had been torn from my body by a Kraut machine-gunner in the mass grave of Somme-Py. Exorbitant pains gushed from my stump. It was rising, increasing in intensity, fanning out, pulling and tearing me in every direction, causing me to torque as if I were fired by an internal furnace being stoked inside and torn, as if by a circular saw. Out of the void, I was seized by a sense of being reborn ceaselessly. It was a stupefying sensation that thrust me outside of myself and troubled my most elementary reflexes, disorientated me, unbalanced me and caused me to lose the exact notion of my corporeal dimensions.[7]

Fever, exhaustion, the bottle of cognac that I had swilled down in one draught, the jolts and bumps of the road, the horror, the terror

---

7. New discreet allusion to the secret of the invalid divinified by his wound; This theme appears again in "Sky" (1949).

of being shuttled about like livestock. Then, there was the stench—the foul, pestiferous stench and the gagging brought on by chloroform or camphor oil, the hunger, the fatigue, the sensations, the vertigo of being in free fall, the bombings, the insults, the pure misery, the gunfire from the attack, the bombs, the explosions, the back-and-forth incessant relentlessness of battle, the rat-a-tat of German machine-guns massacring us in our barbed-wire coffins. The man whom I had garrotted with a thrust of my knife, my severed arm, the screams of friends. Then, this abyssal, infernal longing to get myself out of there and live, to live and exult again! That fleeting wish crushed by a series of images—of the thousands of wounded men, of surgeons alongside us in the field where I had so recently fought, the blood pissing out of me and others, the cold that overtook me. Then the sudden onset of another fear—of falling asleep, of fainting and dying without even noticing it, the terror of being forgotten … all of this fed my delirium. My last defences had been breached, and my muted soul suddenly found voice. I started screaming and shouting for help with all my strength in this rich, beautiful, and austere ecclesiastical residence. But, maybe I had only imagined myself screaming with everything I had; I could just as easily have been barely breathing or weakly moaning or whingeing, scarcely able to aspirate because I was expiring. In any case, I recall being delivered into a savage, long and sinister battle so as not to lose consciousness, for to surrender was to fall into a coma, patiently waiting in the shadows to envelop me.

At one point, a church bell rang and buzzed in my ears. Or maybe it was that just before our departure, before pinching the tarp, the driver who had abandoned me in this sumptuous hall had started ringing the bell or had spoken to me of a bell to ring to summon others to come. That was it! I recall that at a given time, a bell was ringing, or the notion of a bell was reverberating in my heat-oppressed brain. I desperately tried to get up and pull on the tongue inside this bell hanging somewhere in the corner of the deserted hall. I knew this bell was a phantom. It had to be a phantom, and yet! I heard it, on several occasions, ringing—*gong, gong, gong!*—in my head, and each time, my despair was infinite to see that this bell pushing me to the far fringes of sanity had not disturbed so much as a single soul's tranquillity.

So, there I was, face-to-face, in a partial embrace with the angel of death who was preparing to liquify me into the sky above and tuck my head into her soft and warm plumage, the better to asphyxiate me. I had already divined her presence enveloping my physical surroundings that were becoming increasingly blurred and unhinged, when I noticed, suddenly, a quiver of a robe, the vibration of a rosary and miniature medals and like mice nibbling in the silence, a furtive step that glided in the stairwell. And my attention was drawn by a hand that had rested, above, all the way in the heights, on the sombre rail of the stairs at the first stairhead and making her out as she descended the final steps. A woman dressed in black and coiffed with the fluttering wings of a nun's cornet, Sister Philomène, whose step slowed the closer she approached me, and who froze on the penultimate step, the time to sigh, "O mother Maria, a naked man!" and brought her hands to the heart and fell—all of her—across my stretcher.

* * *

Poor Sister Philomène, so gentle, so attentive, so stubborn in the prayers that she came after that to recite each night in my chamber of the grievously wounded, as one prays for an exorcism. I think that she could never vanquish the fright that the sight of me had caused her the night of my arrival at the hospital. Looking back, she must have been ashamed of her weakness.

"It is not the blood, covering you from head to foot, that caused me fear, my poor friend, but your abandonment; I did not see the man, but the mortal ... the mortal sinner ..."

"You are correct, Sister, because I have killed.[8] Today, there were millions of us, all brandishing weapons."

---

8. "I have killed": echo of the brief and violent piece published by Cendrars in 1918.

But Sister Philomène didn't come to pray in my room or to converse with me. She possessed her truth. So, as soon as I opened my mouth, she withdrew, retreating while enveloping me with signs of the cross that appeared like calligraphy or butterflies on an ancient scroll.

* * *

Part III: The Death Of The Little Shepherd

The sisters kept vigil over us at night, and registered nurses of the *Association des Femmes de France* tended to our wounds during the day.

The upper storey of the bishopric had been converted into a *lazaretto*, initially designed to receive 150 to 200 seriously wounded cases, but in the wake of the failed Champagne offensive, there were 500 of us.

Nurse Major Mme Adrienne was responsible for these pathetic victims, churned out on the death assembly line by the weapons and the surgery of automatized wars—a woman with a grand heart.

I remained in the hospital in Châlons-sur-Marne for nearly a month, and I had more than enough time to observe that our infirmary's devotion was boundless.

Mme Adriene P … gave of herself to her terrible and often repugnant medical tasks with such verve, tact and delicacy, and with such dexterity and attention to the tiniest details in the care she brought with firm kindness. And, I haven't mentioned the gifts, the sweets and delicacies, the acts of kindness and attentiveness that she showered upon her dear wounded. It must also have cost her a pretty penny (which, in turn, no doubt, must have put a grievous dent into her meagre purse). First and foremost, each of us, who only escaped through great suffering from the killing fields and were still muddied from the trenches, gained the impression, which became a conviction, that he was the favourite preferred son of this woman, jealous of her little ones. As I say, each of us felt especially spoiled, pampered, and morally supported and comforted by this volunteer nurse. In addition to her other duties, her charitable activity even went so far as to serve as secretary for correspondence with families. God knows that these letters from pulverized, shattered *poilus*[9] in the flower of their youth were rude confessions, loaded with pitiless accusations and foul imprecations sent to parents, masters, the motherland, or the beloved wife, regrets, considerations on life, despair, upsetting and overwhelming desires, childish confessions, troubling admissions, lies due to pride that the Nurse unveiled and brought into the daylight ... none of this facilitated the correspondence of this voluntary, lucid, attentive and courageous witness who remained sensitive and overextended, who had to transmit hélas! often on the day after the initial news of a serious wound, the announcement of a fatal outcome and as expressions, wishes of condolences, last wishes, i.e. nine times out of ten, the curse of a soldier who had been sacrificed, but who had defended even into the wee minutes preceding his death, vehemently, passionately, his desperate desire to be a hero.

At the bishopric, the upper mezzanine wounded had such a devotion for their nurse that I saw men with trepanned skulls smiling. The mad and the trauma cases were becalmed, and they even acted carefree. The feverish fell silent; the agitated mastered themselves; one-legged men ran too fast on their crutches to please Mme Adrienne and to compensate her. I saw dying men rise to a sitting position, put on a show, greet, pay homage, and affirm clearly that they were finally out of the game and could ease into death with elegance. But I also saw Mme Adrienne P ..., after her day of exhausting labour, spending entire nights at the bedside of one of these miserable, banged-up cases who were brought to her daily from the front and dropped in their soiled stretchers in a small, padded cell, because their condition was desperate and because their distraught bawling was even more odious than their lacerated flesh. I watched our nurse implore the surgeons to attempt the impossible, fight the entire night, syringe in hand. I watched her dose the morphine to soothe the pain of a martyrized soldier. Or I'd hear

---

9. Legionnaires.

her stifled sobs when the heart of a man failed and when the unknown soldier, matriculated but anonymous, trespassed from life into the beyond.

Her gift of herself was whole, unrestricted, unreserved, and absolute. Mme Adrienne P … tended to each of her wounded in the operating room. She personally and tirelessly applied the most complicated and most excruciatingly painful dressings. At the same time, she wouldn't even leave anyone else on the funeral cortege to administer the deceased's makeup. She would watch over the body in the chapel. Then, she would accompany the remains to the cemetery, no longer as a dignified carer but as a woman in mourning frock and veil, paying her final respects. Each time she returned from a burial, silent, then losing her footing, collapsing under her veils, letting herself go as a mother who has just lost her only son—and then, if her ward so allowed, she came to seek refuge inside my room. She spoke to me of her profound chagrin. During those days, since we quickly became the closest of friends, this courageous woman whom the entire hospital admired confessed to me the mortal weariness, the neurasthenia, the disgust that had silently crept into her ardent soul. She had no shame in tucking up her skirts in my presence while conjuring up two or three shots of caffeine to regain her energy and remain up to the task she imposed upon herself, and to prevent her energy and nerves from betraying her.

"It's not that I am a wife, daughter, granddaughter, or great-granddaughter of French officers or that I don't have children," she said one day. My husband was unfortunate enough to serve in Paris's back offices. I believe that my duty was to come to the front lines. And what shouldn't we do to save our honour and even France itself, Monsieur Cendrars?"

If I don't hold women in contempt, maybe it's because I've known her and met two or three other nurses of the same calibre during the war, all of whom were prepared to pay for their beliefs by placing themselves in the greatest danger conceivable.

* * *

Like a miser hoarding his treasure, Mme Adriene P ... jealously guarded certain wounded and let nobody else approach them. She even disputed the regimental surveillance of the doctors and military surgeons that she found far too invasive.

These select wounded were installed in a suite of housekeeping rooms, narrow as cells. The only security she hadn't implemented was locking them up lock-and-key.

I wasn't part of her select group, although Mme Adrienne spoiled me in a very particular way. Every morning, she'd bring me deluxe cigarettes—golden-tipped Muratti-Lauristons—at noon, a few flowers (which she no doubt ordered from Paris), during the day, books (the works of Gringore, Saint-Amant, Scarron[10]), coming to keep me company as soon as she had a break—making small talk, lingering for that little extra moment, taking pleasure in prodding me into recounting my adventures in China or America. I forgot her lassitude but did not allow anyone to dress or unwrap my bandage. And what indeed was my simple, my healthy amputation compared with the multiple wounds, the complicated fractures, the inexplicable trepanations, the insidious infections of respiratory airways, the blindness, the mental and functional troubles of the gas victims, the smashed-in faces, the trauma cases, the paralytics, the dazed and dumb, those who inhabited the corridors of angst, the blind who, by her nocturnal vigils, consistency, stubbornness, audacity, inventive genius, divination in the daily tender care of all instants, also from her heart, prayers, appeals, patience, love, tenderness, maternal protection, this woman bit by bit coaxed back from the brink of death or despair?

One day, Mme Arienne came looking for me: "I hope I wasn't mistaken, Cendrars, in coming to find you. I have been tending to a poor little shepherd from the Landes who is suffering terribly. I am going to move you to his room. You will keep all your books and

---

10. The readings of the war casualty leave little room for modern literature: Gringore (1475–1538), Saint-Amant (1594–1661), Scarron (1610–1660) were nevertheless, each in his way, writers on the margins of the institution—as was their reader.

other pastimes, but I am counting on you to distract him. This will not amuse you because the poor child is an orphan. He doesn't speak much, so you will have to attend to his bandage, which covers a terrible wound. At least once per day. Engage with him and tell him stories that will make him feel good. You will excuse me, won't you, Cendrars?"

This poor beggar of a shepherd from the Landes was an insignificant, anonymous nobody of a soldier. What we call a *bleuet*, classe 15, whom some ordnance had riddled with shrapnel before they had even designated his dugout, even before he had time to place his rucksack on the ground and to scope the layout to find out for himself about these famous trenches the whole country was talking about. Walnut-brown hair and eyebrows furrowed. His face was gaunt, cheeks hollow. Now prone. Head down, the face of this adolescent disappeared almost entirely under his pillow covers. His suffering creased his features, and when the pain caused him to bawl out, his lips receded and exposed the teeth of a young wolf. A vein that ludicrously inflated out at the root of the nose blocked his forehead, and his nostrils pinched. He closed his eyes, and an anguished sweat covered his neck and temples.

He was a taciturn boy. Our beds nearly touched in the narrow small room, if I can give the name of bed to the ramshackle contraption built where the unfortunate soul was suspended by belts, hoops, straps and a rack-and-pinion system like a yoked ox, and his buttocks in the air, already for forty-nine days!

He had already received 72 shells in the lower kidney area, which had naturally created 72 deep wounds of varying dimensions. One was a large round hole that had run through him laterally from one side to the other. This meant he was being infected by seeping faecal matter. It's hard to say how many kilos of iron, misshapen forms, saw-toothed chunks, shrapnel in packs of fine needles had invaded his body. Then, a rather extraordinary thing. A one-hundred-sou coin. This is what had created the big round hole infecting him—a coin that the poor little shepherd boy of the Landes declared he didn't have in his pocket when he was hit, being an orphan, without anybody, without even a war foster mother, and having never dreamt of being able to have in his hands one day such a sum.

He was operated on a good dozen times, with yet more surgery on the horizon due to this infection that was spreading and fresh shrapnel ploughing into his flesh that had to be ceaselessly extracted. It was crazy what this little soldier had to endure over 24 hours, even if he was sedated. Since he was feverish at night, the approach of that time brought on mounting agitation and delirium. But the most atrocious moment of the day was for him when the bandage had to be changed. The bandage weighed on his conscience like original sin and caused him an unholy dread. When the time approached, and we heard the medics and nurses approaching in the corridor, he would begin screaming, terrorized in anticipation of what awaited him.

I was sorely tempted to leave off with the description of this torture chamber that I was obliged to revisit every day, since that moment that Mme Adrienne had persuaded me to share the field of dreams of this stranded piece of human shrapnel. In hindsight, I still get the shakes when I recall it. Suffice to record that it was necessary to extract 72 threads the size of candle wicks from 72 deep lesions, suture them anew, one after another, wash everything in bleach water, eliminate, dig to the bottom, clean, rinse with saline solution, reapply the dressing, then start working on the transversal hole made by the hundred-sou coin. Pull out the drain, probe, perform injections, cut, pinch, puncture, extract, fray, pour iodine tincture into the hole, reposition and place the drain, and bandage this pathetic, squalling body. Then, shake him, flip him over, change his position, re-strap him, clean and bathe him, redo the bed, and that took three hours on the clock every afternoon. It was so complicated. The surgeon departed with his claw forceps, scrapers and clamps as soon as he performed his task. The attendant physician was just as eager to disappear as quickly as he had done his injections and jabs, prescribed drugs and medication, and diet. It fell to Mme P ..., upon this poor friend Adrienne as an executioner who has to automatically carry out his dire duty, to go and pursue, with a steady hand, the follow-up of this cruel treatment. I confess that she managed the job with art and dexterity until, job done, her gaze returned to mine.

"You can now understand, Monsieur Cendrars, why I am disgusted," she commented as she sat on my bed. "I can't take it any longer. Still, I'm so proud of this little man. I'm the one who set him up there and obtained this treatment. They wanted to butcher him, and I wanted to save him. I know it's painful for him, and he has a long road ahead. But, my dear friend, if you only knew by what paths this poor little man has already passed. He was condemned. Ten, twenty times, the doctors wanted to abandon him, saying that there was nothing more to do, that the infection was in the ascendancy. But, we both resisted, and now, I can assure you, he's already improving, and the surgeon himself admits that his case is no longer a desperate one ...

An odour of rot, camphor, phenol, Peru balsam and excrement reigned in the sweltering, cramped, minuscule room. The little shepherd from the Landes, his bandages redressed, lying like a sacrificial lamb whimpering and bleating at the altar. Mme Adrienne P ... bowed her head on my shoulder, and I caressed her hands with my remaining hand.

"I admire you, and I pity you," I said.

But Mme Adrienne was already on her way out, responding to the cries of the countless others wounded.

My severed arm was ready to torment me anew.

"Dirty goddam war!" I yelled out to nobody.

* * *

Despite the individual dramas playing out in every last bed of this extreme emergency lazaret, games of life and death that are the humdrum routine of a hospital, time passed relatively easily at the bishopric of Châlons-sur-Marne, mainly because mankind has an uncanny knack for getting used to pretty much anything, even an unworthy thing to have to confess, even not being respected in his physical integrity.

This thought is abominable to me, and to not feel physically diminished by the amputation of my right arm, after several days of hospitalization, I devised a plan. As soon as possible, I'd prop myself up in bed every morning at dawn and box for a quarter of an hour into my pillow slip. My arm bled abundantly, but I took no account of it, overcoming the pain of punching with my stump, applying twice the force with increasing speed.

On the nineteenth day, the surgeon attributed the record healing of my arm to this repeated exercise. The healing of the scar surprised him to the point that he adopted a new guideline for amputees—to engage in the same type of exercise. I credit boxing for allowing me to believe that, even if I was no longer whole, I had physical equilibrium again.

After boxing, I started juggling in my bed with oranges and small objects, learning to use my left hand with strength, then with dexterity, and using my truncated right arm to launch a ball or to hold a plate, glasses, or a vase in equilibrium. And, as always, for the same reason, not to feel physically diminished, once I returned to civilian life, I would begin practising all the rough-and-tumble sports and games of skill like football, swimming, mountain-climbing, horseback riding, tennis, basketball, or billiards, pétanque, pistol-shooting, fencing, croquet, darts, thanks to which today, I can now drive my race car as well as I can type or write left-handed, which brings me joy.

Joy was the last thing on my mind in that hospital bed. When I delivered myself up to my first exercises, I found childish pleasure in seeing that I wasn't too clumsy. Besides, the little shepherd whom Mme Adrienne had assigned to me derived far more enjoyment from my tricks as a juggler or tightrope walker than from my stories.

Poor little man! This little shepherd of the Landes taught me that the human spirit can comprehend the infinite when—or who knows—maybe because the human body's pain is also infinite. The horror of life itself is also unlimited and fathomless.

Part IV: A Very Elegant Homicide

Wretched bastard!

One afternoon, around 4 pm, they had just completed the final swaddling of the bandage of the little shepherd, and my bed partner lay in a state of exhaustion, stunned by a massive dose of *pantonpon*. I was reading serenely when a rumour was being relayed through the rooms and the corridors that a famous physician, one of the masters of the Academy, director of God knows what hospital of Paris, and if memory serves me correctly, must have been called something like Monsieur the honourable Professor Van Ditch or Mac-Trench, in other words, a real big shot, general's stripes to boot, was coming to the bishopric. Sainte-Croix was turned upside down as soon as the news of this inspection was announced.

All we could hear was staff running up and down the corridors, voices shouting, orders, chairs being tossed about, beds being moved around in the neighbouring rooms. The nurses entered and left, changed the bedsheets, brought in fresh towels and pillow slips, turned up hospital corners and thwacked the sheets, arranged vases, flagons and trays, and brought in toilet pails. Everything that was hanging about—clothes, crutches, treats, hobbies, card games, books, magazines, newspapers, user manuals, faded flowers, old cigar boxes with war souvenirs of the *poilus,* uniform buttons, epaulette straps, German chargers, alumni rings, lighters made from cartridges, love letters, photos, etc. etc.—was given the once-over. Auxiliary house-keeping women entered and left on their heels to wipe down, feather, polish, air out rooms, crease out the folds of curtains, empty ashtrays and the aubergines.

Convalescents slid furtively from a room in an alcove, hyper-excited by the news that they peddled, announcing the general evacuation from the hospital, the moving out to hotels on the Riviera or the immediate implementation of a reform of all these poor buggers, sensational news that the big-shot physician was going to confirm *illico presto*. But, if some of these tinkerers were as joyful as children for their imminent demobilization and their upcoming family reunions, in which they believed in good faith, others, either more astute or more sceptical, went back to bed, absorbing as much as they could of any available plonk, *apéros*, spirits, medication to create a fever, scratched themselves, ready to re-infect wounds and scars, not to excite the pity of anybody or to even leave the good life of the hospital, but because they knew that the arrival of top brass was not good news for a soldier. These long-toothed, dog-faced bastards kept their counsel, ready to convince anybody that they stood at the brink of death and even regretting that all four of their limbs hadn't been amputated.

In the middle of all this hurly-burly, Madame Adrienne appeared, having come from her home in the city at our request.

"I am very vexed, Cendrars," she remarked while moving through the room after having cast an anxious glance toward the little shepherd dulled with fatigue. "Shh, he is sleeping! I have just learned that we have received the order to unravel all the bandages. *Monsieur l'inspecteur* wishes to see our wounded, one at a time. He is a general. He is going to arrive at any moment now. And I can't possibly inflict this torment upon this poor little man a second time in the day! He won't survive it. What can I do?"

"My God, Madame P ... turn out the lights and lock the door to our room."

"That's impossible."

"Then, have him start his visit at the other end of the hospital and lead the celebrated professor everywhere, in the kitchen, in the laundry room, down in the cellars. Show him the pharmacy, the autoclaves, and the cupboards; don't hide anything. Take him for a stroll in all the corners and niches, and maybe this General will want to leave, and if it's late, he might forget us, the two of us. It's already later than four o'clock. Surely, he doesn't want to sleep here, no? In an hour or two, he'll have had his fill. Let everything lag; delay wherever you can."

"You're probably right. But you don't know the inspectors from the health department. They're going to dig around everywhere, obviously, but it's mainly for our poor, little wounded boys that I'm worried. So long as something unfortunate doesn't occur! I'm frighteningly worried. Just think, if he comes to a halt in front of him, and he starts demanding how, why, and this and that, then, worst of all, he decides that he wants to do something about it! …"

"But no, no, Madame. You're getting all worked up. You exaggerate. What can a General do to such a poor little waif? In his condition, he won't even look at him. At any rate, you'll be there, and if he wants to touch him, the surgeon and you, you will have to tell him that it's impossible. That you cannot do two bandage changes in a single day. That would be too horrific. Come to think of it, show him his body temperature readings. He had another feverish surge only today. By God, this general is a physician, isn't he? He'll understand."

"Do you really think so?"

"Naturally! Listen, my friend. Don't touch the little man. But you can undo my bandage to show that my arm is healed, and when I hear him coming, this grand ogre of a General, I'll park myself in the doorway to stop him from coming and tell him how well you have treated me."

"I forbid you to get out of your bed, Cendrars!"

"Why wouldn't I? Just find me any old smock since I arrived here naked, and I don't even have a uniform, and you'll see! You know well, Adrienne, that the surgeon can't believe that the scar on my arm is already healing. He figures it's a record! So, today, I will put on a real show for him. I'll stand up, I swear to you, and I'll receive him in full pomp, him and his general. I'll salute the President of the Republic if he shows up! …"

* * *

I didn't want to start bragging, and on top of that, I had overestimated my strength. As soon as the Nurse Major had left, and I tried to stand up alone, I had to stretch myself out on the waxed flooring, falling with my entire weight on my severed arm, which triggered a blast of pain worse than on the day I was wounded on the battlefield by a spray of machine-gun fire. Even so, when Mme Adrienne returned several instants later with an enormous bathrobe that she'd gone to hunt down for me, she found me tottering to attention, clinging to the bars of my bed. By 5 pm, I had taken several steps into the room, and Mme P ..., although far from convinced of the fate of her little shepherd, was at least reassured by me. She left to meet the General, whose arrival had just been announced by a bell.

At six pm, I started to feel my support in my foot.

By seven pm, I was slumped on a chair, feeling slightly seasick, and everything was starting to oscillate around me.

At eight pm, I was flat on my back in bed but ready to leap up at the first alert when someone arrived to announce that dinner was about to be served.

Life had already been suspended four hours on the clock for this General, whose inspection was endless and utterly disrupted the hospital services' scheduling and functioning.

Sometime between eight and nine pm, chaos. Temperatures had yet to be taken, and the 500 wounded being treated received a cold meal served in haste by the kitchen girls. I learned through this staff that, upon arrival, a tempestuous session had taken place in the office of the Intendant, and the General had been bawling out surgeons, doctors and nurses. Everybody was on a knife's edge.

At the shift change, the nuns informed me that the famous Parisian surgeon was locked inside the operating room and, for the last two or three hours, was sawing off arms and legs to show the medical staff what was what in the bishopric. Everybody was upset and dead worried. In all the rooms, the wounded were getting frantic, and generally, the temperature was skyrocketing upwards.

A bit later, Sister Philomène, spotting me from the head of the stairwell, came to tell me "that they were all feasting, the General, the intendant, the doctors and the lay nurses, "that they didn't seem to be bored, judging from the raucous laughter audible from the ground-floor dining room, where the doors were locked to anyone outside. Sister Philomène appeared indignant.

It could have been ten-thirty or forty-five when my roommate, who had remained drowsy until then, opened his eyes and asked, "Tell me, old man, what's going on?"

"What?"

"What's with all the noise?"

"What are you talking about?"

"All the racket!"

"What do you mean? You're hallucinating."

"Then ... why didn't anyone take my temperature this evening?"

"You slept."

"Then ... why haven't I been served dinner?"

"I'm telling you, you were sleeping. I told them to leave you alone, seeing you were snoozing in la-la land for once."

"... Tell me, old man. I had a helluva nightmare."

"Ah!"

"Yes, ah! ... I dreamt that that ... tell me, you don't believe I'm going down, do you? ... I dreamt that I was going to bite it, and now, I'm not sure anymore that I'll make it ..."

"You're talking like a moron."

"You're talking straight? ... Then, tell me, why didn't Mme Adrienne come this evening, like she always does? I'm not going down? Tell me I'm not going down, Cendrars."

"Mme Adrienne? Is that what you're worried about? She'll be around. I'm waiting for her myself. I even got dressed for the occasion. Listen, we'll do a bit of a practical joke on her. It'll crack you up."

My roommate turned with difficulty. I stood up in the huge bathrobe that she had draped over me as if I were a statue of Balzac.[11] The little man searched my gaze.

"... It's so strange, so strange ...," he stammered. "You look so big ... tell me, Cendrars, what is happening?"

"What do you mean?"

---

11. This refers to Rodin's statue of Balzac, today situated on the corner of boulevard Raspail and boulevard du Montparnasse in Paris.

"I don't understand ... Why are you clothed? ... You're not leaving me, are you?"

At the end of a long silence, the tormented soul asked me, increasingly angst-ridden: "... But, wait, what time is it? ... can you hear them? ... You'd think they were coming ..."

He was right about something. There was a fair bit of noise coming from the corridor.

Right away, the little Landais shepherd began shrieking with terror.

"Ah! ... Oh! ... No! ... I don't want to. I don't want to! ... Mme Adrienne! ... I beg you! ... I'm too young to die! Ah! ... Oh! ..."

He had gone completely mad.

"What is going on?"

A booming voice.

A group now invaded our room. Eleven o'clock had just sounded.

* * *

"So, it's you making all the racket?" said a broad-shouldered man in a white shirt, shoving me back from the doorway.

Mme Adrienne, our surgeon, the doctors nurses, other members of the night and evening shifts, including military nurses pushing gauze and bandage carts, made up the entourage escorting this large jovial man, with the kepi trimmed with gold braid, plunked diagonally on his skull, revealing his congested face, dented forehead, the bulging veins on his temples, the groomed moustache, the browned teeth, and the small, fiercely laughing, but sharp, agate-tinted eyes.

"My General," I said. "I am cured! My arm's wound has sealed off and formed a scar. I'm moving it. You know, I can already juggle and box with it. And I've only been here three weeks. I was wounded on 29 September. It's a record!"

I started juggling three tennis balls I had ready for my performance.

The inspector burst out laughing.

"But that's marvellous, my friend; now go lay down. But, now, your friend, hanging there, what has he got?" he inquired of Mme Adrienne, who had raced to bedside to protect her pint-sized martyr.

The Nurse Major set to providing background explanations of the wounds, the extraction of the innumerable bits of shrapnel, the story of the hundred-sou coin, providing particulars on the treatment applied, the appropriate and delicate care to fight the infection, the suffering endured by the patient who was improving so steadily that the surgeon had confirmed that he was now on the verge of turning the corner for the best. The General listened to her attentively, but the little shepherd was braying like a jackass: "Ah! Oh! ..." without saying anything else.

The room was bursting with personnel.

By this time, I was back sitting on my bed.

"Give him the temperature sheet," I whispered to Sister Philomène, standing before me.

"Take off his bandages," the Professor ordered. "I want to examine him."

"No! No!" the kid screamed.

"Don't worry," Mme Adrienne said to the little man, who was contorting, bawling, and struggling while she worked to remove the bandages. It's nothing, my child. It won't take a second, and it's for your good. You'll see."

"Hurry up," the General urged while he and the surgeon slipped on their rubber gloves. The bandage cart was wheeled close. It was used as a bed rack to keep the wounded shepherd in proper posture, and the circle of the curious came closer so as not to miss any of the utterances of the famous practitioner of Paris.

Mme Adrienne cast me a desperate glance.

The Inspector General now held pliers and a lancet. He ripped off the strips roughly, one by one, leaned onto the perforated buttocks, smelled them up close, probing each wound, then, without so much as an acknowledgement of the inhuman screams of the peasant, removed the drain from the large lateral hole, scoured it, stood up, and frowned:

"Congratulations, Madame, I admire your courage. But this method won't get you anywhere. It's a labour of patience, a real puzzle, but you're losing time. All these wasps' nests are dens of infection, so these temperature fluctuations and volatile jumps in the curve occur. What you think you have earned one day is lost ground the next because the field is mined. What is it? We are on a battlefield. The ground is mined. Therefore, we cannot wait and remain at the enemy's mercy. We must beat the clock, outwit the enemy, outrace him. We cannot dither, trying this path one day and another the next. We must do some rearguard sabotage to obtain a result brutally and by ambush. Pass me my scalpel. *Non, merci.* I won't worry about surface funnels, as deep as they are. The danger is not there, But I must detect the main site of infection, the blast furnace that can erupt in our faces and play a dirty trick on us sooner or later. So, we have to bring together all these funnels and retrace a network of casings that all feed a principal trench. That will allow us to create a deep irrigation canal and flush out the enemy everywhere he hides. There is no traffic jam on the ground that is so bottled up that one need surrender. Rather, a grand boulevard that leads to a central locus of the problem. You heard me. A one-way road with a single entrance and a single exit. We cut an incision, yet another, very deep, and here we are in the sapper's trench as in a central sewage system, under the *place de l'Opéra*. With the entire surface being drained, we can direct our full attention to the centre, which, now cleared in-depth, is accessible. I apply a staple in the upper area; it closes it off. I ..."

Having accompanied his words with deeds, the eminent professor of the faculty who was holding forth for the gallery as before an auditorium giving his lectures, before a public of students, carved him open, re-sutured the 72 wounds lesions, that he launched into a single, wide, deep wound, that he had carved out in such a beautiful channel that, after fifty minutes of demonstration, the soldier was dead. But by then, the Landes soldier had ceased complaining for quite some time.

* * *

Part V: Vesti La Giubba

At the end of my sojourn in the Châlons-sur-Marne hospital, I had the opportunity to witness an authentic resurrection in another small room in the bishopric's loft, where Mme Adrienne had again placed me, again under the pretext that I was a positive influence.

The wounded man with whom I was now keeping company was a gargantuan sergeant, so ungainly, so tall and of such a massive girth that while we couldn't reinforce him, we could at least add an extension to his bed to support his feet, which stuck out at the end.

This colossus had been trepanned once and then a second time. After the first time, he remained paralyzed on the right side. Then, after the second time, he lost the power of speech. He was an over-sized docile puppet, gluttonous and clumsy, who spilled his soup on the bedsheets and lapsed into ridiculous temper tantrums whenever anyone wanted to touch the husky gunner's greatcoat that was used on his bed because, inside the folds of it, there was a brand new *Légion d'honneur* cross that this baby-adult incubated. His eyes and numb fingers caressed it ceaselessly until he fell into sleep—like the way a newborn uses his rattle.

It was pretty pathetic to watch Mme Adrienne, who came several times daily to sit at his bedside, re-educate this musclebound, solid and well-proportioned man. She retrained him in the use of his limbs by placing a glass ball in the hollow of his hand, pronouncing distinctively and with insistency the words: "ball-round-cold," searching in his intelligent eyes for a sign that these words awakened a notion within his cognition or presented to him an alphabet in colours and tried to have him read, to say with her, following the letters, the syllables of the finger, B-A-BA = BABA. T-O-TO = TOTO, R-I-RI = RIRI. Etc.

"Have you noticed his eyes, Cendrars, when a glint illuminates them?" Mme Adrienne said after each session. "He has been making great progress since you arrived, you know. I am sure he will now understand everything that was said to him. Soon, he will speak."

And the nurse would depart, full of faith and set about her other business, only to return two, three hours after having again made the man-doll smile and recommencing to re-teach him from square one with a marvellous, angelic, inexhaustible and radiant patience.

* * *

This gunner was an extremely handsome man with very regular features of great distinction, and the bandage that crowned his head, far from dimming or darkening them, added an indefinable radiance and nobility. Rendered fragile by his wound, he resembled a Byzantine, turbaned prince. Even his blunders—more due to weariness than paralysis —did not wholly ravish his natural elegance. I found myself more inclined to attribute this prostrate man's hesitant manners and clumsy postures to an imperial awkwardness—and the little catastrophes which flowed from him and because his brain, deflowered by a foreign body, had been altered by the scalpel. His eyes were more lively, mobile, and eloquent; they expressed an entire gamut of things.

It was extraordinary and, for me, a pleasure ceaselessly renewed. It often occasionally provoked ecstasy within me when I succeeded and contemplated his expressive eyes, to decode, to divine, to comprehend what his gaze meant in a flash.

How can one express so many things with one's eyes? I don't mean moral or abstract things because my interrogation didn't extend so far, but more the obscure needs for organic functions and the quasi-vegetative life that, in the ordinary course of events, barely reach the periphery of our consciousness, but are repressed or indecent to repeat. Yet the gaze of this mutilated casualty with the perforated skull somehow allowed me to understand that he was hungry, thirsty or had to relieve himself.

Mme Adrienne was right. There was enormous progress because, since the time that I shared his room, this half-paralyzed, wounded man tracked me with his eyes while I moved around him, juggled, boxed, delivering myself up to all sorts of exercises of flexibility, suppleness and balance while continually speaking to him to attract his attention, no longer wet or soiled his garments, save in the night.

* * *

One night—in the pre-dawn—I awoke with a start.

My neighbour was seated on his bed, greatcoat, sheets, and cover torn apart and tossed to the ground.

I don't know how he pulled it off, but the paralytic was now firmly upright. His eyes resembled two death stars. They were shining. He was undertaking desperate efforts; his jaw contracted, the throat pulsating, the mouth agape, trying to say something—a word that he had at the tip of his tongue, at the edge as if trying to escape the buccal gate, but that he still wasn't managing to expel from inside.

Immediately, I rang the alarm. I called out, and then I ran into the corridor; I alerted everyone, and in no time at all, Sister Philomène, the other sisters, the porter and the night nurse, the on-duty medic and the surgery team surrounded the bed of the handsome gunner who, through mounting tension, the pectorals, the bulging muscles, strained tautly with all his being. His will was visibly being pushed to the extreme. He remained there, mouth agape, the tragic mask theatrical, the eyes bulging with desire, still unable to release the gas from within.

Two or three hours passed, and everyone anxiously wondered what was going to happen when, around 7 a.m., Mme Adrienne had gone to awaken him. Seeing his nurse enter the room, the voice triumphant, the eyes revolving, transported and fainting, our gentle, child giant cooing: CA-CA = CACA! before slackening. And while everyone fussed around him, Mme P ... crazy with joy, wrapped her arms around my neck.

"It's the most beautiful day of my life, Blaise! He spoke. Now, he is saved. Thank you. Thank you."

And me? I was very embarrassed, at a loss for words, not only because Sister Philomène was watching us, but because I didn't feel

I deserved the compliments from this mistress/woman to whom I owed the first hours of quietude and joy since the beginning of this war, but because for the first time in my life, I was hugging a woman with only one arm.

So, to avoid feeling this embarrassment and the astonishment of everyone, I took the nurse major through three or four tours of a swaying waltz, singing:

"*Je n'ai dansé qu'une fois avec elle ...*[12])

"Adrienne, thank you, thank you from all of us. We love you ... all of us!"[13]

---

12. This song also appears in *The Severed Hand* (*La Main coupée* (1917))
13. This "word of life" according to Yvette Bozon-Scalzitti, recalls "the resurrection of Saturnin in the *Aurélia* of de Nerval—that Cendrars borrowed and the remainder of the first names of the female characters in his novel, *Philomène et Adrienne.*" (*Blaise Cendrars ou la passion de l'écriture*, l'Age de L'homme, 1977, p. 127)

THE CIRCLE OF
THE DIAMOND[1]

I

YOU CAN RECOGNIZE the blue diamond, the diamond of Brazil, because certain stones emit a fiery reflection and illuminate the night sky even though they do not reflect any light source.

I am speaking of a raw diamond, such as you find in the stony slopes or *cascalho*[2] on the banks of the river, after one of these violent storms that burst out daily as night falls at the approach of the rainy season in this torrid zone of the great Brazilian forest, when the black swarms of the tornado retreat, obstructing the sky and rendering the tropical night opaque and impenetrable.

It is right at this time that you can see within a pile of stones and sand heaped during the day by diamond hunters on the right bank of this river, lost in the confines of the virgin forests of Matto Grosso and Goyaz, and which bears the name of *Rio das Garças*, which is to say the river of the Egrets, a small glistening in the darkness, haloed with a phosphorescent circle, emitting a soft blue light.

---

1. This story first appeared as a "True tale" in *Paris-Soir Dimanche* n° 80, July 4, 1937.
2. *Cascalho*: "loose stones": "Bed of coarse calcium (tertiary) mixed with marl, silicium, sand, gypsum. The hope of finding diamonds and other precious stones pushed adventurers to join in waves of migration to the interior of the country." (Mariza Veiga, *Le Lexique brésilien de Blaise Cendrars*, Nice, Centre du XXe siècle, 1977)

A diamond has just been born ...

* * *

After exposure to a day's worth of warm rainfall, a particular stone that doesn't usually stand out suddenly gives off a nascent glint in the darkness. It appears as though the stone has been naturally cleansed of its muddy exterior. It is not rare, even in mid-day, to see other detached stones glistening from the river water. These diamonds have been deposited inside the silt at its bottom, from where they shimmer beneath the eddies, particularly in the gloom upstream of the larger rocks that block the current. But this description shouldn't lead you to conclude that the trade of the diamond digger is a trade of a hustler out for quick money.

On the contrary, it is one of the most soul-destroying and hellish trades on this earth.

Most of the time, the diamond digger lives under such deprivation that he doesn't even possess his own *tambu*.[3] This is a wooden bowl, the humble, primitive instrument without which he can't do anything since it's an instrument that allows him to "wash" throughout the day loose stone and ballast, sand and the diamond mud that conceals their fortune. Many of these distressed poor companions form groups of two or three and occasionally larger groups to work separately. It is not so much to fight against the dangers of the bush but rather to possess one of these common tools that they do so.

This mud, sand, and loose stone must be extracted, carted, and placed into piles. Under the fiery sun, it's a calvary for the hellishly damned.

The famous *cascalho* comprises shards of a very hard rock that the diamond diggers pound using chisels and hammer strikes in tandem when they are not forced to churn enormous blocks with crowbars until exhaustion. The equally famous *Cadive do diamante*, the Slave of the diamond, is a name the diggers give to the diamantiferous mud. This is due to the brownish residue that they deposit—primo,

---

3. *Tambu*: bamboo.

a sort of shellac in sticks that resembles sealing wax; secondo, a friable substance similar to rice straw; tertio, another material similar to an ox horn—is a heavy mud mixed with sand and crystalline gravel that you find by plunging into the depths of the river and that is filled into leather sacks with a large opening by swimming against the current until exhausted. In this insidious climate, swimming underwater the whole day is no less killing than pounding stones under that same sun.

This is why the rain, tornadoes, and warm water torrents, notwithstanding their miseries and diseases, are welcome in this hell of the *Rio das Garças*. They create work, "cleanse," and deliver to you—giving you that rare chance to make a discovery without too much effort. This type of thing keeps everybody on top of things through stormy nights. And a pox on the man who imprudently fails to respect the fierce law of the diamond diggers and decides to come within three-and-a-half steps of one of these piles liquefying under the rain. The owner of the piles, a sniper in the shadow of his *carbet*,[4] shoots him down with a bullet and without a word of warning.

And, still, we are only at the stage of a raw diamond that shines innocuously in the mud. Only in Rio de Janeiro, Brazil's fantastical capital filled with equally fantastical women, will this humble precious stone finally gleam with all its flames in a beautiful show window lit with electricity once cut. Only then will this blue diamond, the pride of Brazil, be valued at its true worth. Back here, in the forest, there is only a gourd of rot-gut Cuyaba moonshine and a few tins of Japanese food, courtesy of the Syrian hawker when he manages to find his way to these solitary far reaches. Suppose the peddler doesn't show his face. In that case, the digger will lose heart and lose everything playing cards. This is the day when the black dog bites, when he's sick with fever, curses his existence, loathes the diamond, is disgusted by everything, is enraged at the whole world, and starts quarrelling and squabbling with his companions. For a yes or a no, he will pull out a cutter or discharge his shotgun at the closest human target.

---

4. Carbet: Tupi word: shelter.

There are a lot of violent deaths on the right bank of the *Rio das Garças* because, to tell you the truth, the life of a man isn't worth a damn there.

* * *

In 1926, there were one hundred and forty-two of them in the Camp of the Egrets, *coureurs de bois*, desperadoes, deserters, adventurers, for the most part, métis, or at least they were *caboclos*,[5] from inland, afflicted by the wanderlust. The Brazilian peasant, like all bush-cutters and clearers, is a nomad by temperament. But there were two gringos among the group: a beast of a hirsute Englishman who induced others with superstitious terror by his sleight of hand and his skill in cards. And a German, the Baron van Kleinmiche, no other than Otto. This was certified by his business card nailed to the trunk of a giant cedar destroyed by lightning. The seekers of the camp had nicknamed him Jao dos Barros because, as the passerine[6] of the fields that bore his name, this foreigner, who didn't resemble any of them, went to build his hut at a distance; just as he kept his distance from everybody there.

II

As is often the case, I was in Rio[7] for the Carnival the other year, which in itself is a reason to make this city famous like many other marvels.

---

5. Caboclo: Métis who is a cross-breed of European descent and indigenous. Heir of the ancient or unlucky inroads made during recent adventures, the "caboclo "is the crofter primary, serf, who works a strip of a clearing using primitive techniques and manages to survive in a great material and spiritual impoverishment. (M. Veiga, op.cit.)
6. Passerine is a swallow of the region.
7. Cendrars discovered Brazil in 1924 at the invitation of his Paulist friend, Paulo Prado (1869–1943). Businessman, patron of the modernist movement and essayist. He returned twice in 1926 and 1927–28, in his "second spiritual homeland" and his "Utopialand". This passion for Brazil expressed itself in numerous texts: poems (*Feuilles de route*, 1924), novellas in the cycle of the "True Tales", essays (*Aujourd'hui*, 1931); Brazil 1932; *Trop c'est trop*, (1957), memoirs (*Sky*, 1949).

My friend Luiz would find me at the hotel every night and drag me to a popular nightclub.

The club that was the rage was called the Diamond's Club. An American woman had just opened it on a street lined by majestically imperial palm trees. Earlier, this peaceful neighbourhood was Embassy Row, *rua Paysandàçù*. Despite the challenging economic times, the dance club was overflowing because, just like my friend Luiz, all of Rio was in love with the owner.

Edith de Berensdorff's blond beauty and mysterious charisma attracted a bevy of elegant pretenders. But the marquee entertainment that made the success of the Diamond's Club can be attributed to a unique show, where two frenzied bands competed with each other: a 100% American jazz band led by a prestigious trumpet, the stunning, indefatigable Wild Bird from Saint-Louis, and a typically Brazilian orchestra *Los 8 Batutas*, selected and trained by Donga,[8] the soul-stirring popular composer, the ace, in 1930, of the carioca carnaval, and the furious combat that was waged between these two bands of Black musicians of dissimilar origins but such opposing composition and inspiration, where each lusts to get the better of the other. The contrasting rhythms of a *black-bottom* yield to the continuous, irresistible, black magic of a *macumba*.[9] The erotic acceleration, the controlled rhythm of the sambas and *maxixes* cheated the nervous mechanical of the one, two-steps or the delirium of syncopated slides of the blues. The lascivious *lundum*, the concentrated and pent-up melancholic passion of the South-American Blacks fought to triumph over the eccentric *cake-walk*. Finally came a hilarious improvisation, executed by the Black virtuosos of Louisiana, electrifying the dancing couples and intoxicating the crowd. And it was more the music than

---

8. *Donga*, Ernesto Joaquin Maria dos Santos (dit) (1891–1974). Brazilian musician. Author (with Mauro de Almeida) of the first samba recorded in Brazil. In 116, he recorded Pelo Telefone. He travelled throughout the world promoting samba. With Pixinguinha and other musicians of the group "Os otito batutas" in 1922, his show ran for eight months in Paris at the Shéhérazade cabaret. He played with the most celebrated musicians of his times, including Heitor Villa-Lobos and left a luxurious and diverse body of work: sambas, choros and waltzes.

9. *Macumba or candomblé*: "Fetishist ceremony of African origin and Christian influence accompanied by dances and chants to the sound of a drum." (M. Veiga, op.cit.)

the mix of champagne and whisky that had you stumbling out the door, with temples beating, delirious in the early glorious dawns of Rio that gleaned from between the palm trees, surrendering to fatigue, to joy, after we had been in their presence for the entire night, inside this club that is unique in the world. It was a choir of perverse angels or an outburst of demons. Take your pick.

* * *

Like all the foreign women who came to Rio to rebuild their lives, promiscuous women, actresses, intriguers, adventuresses, and who succeeded or failed in varying degrees, Edith de Berensdorff had created her own myth. Since this woman was advertising her origins as being in New York, her legend was necessarily romantic.

Her legion of languorous admirers added to her myth—and each of them wanted to pass himself off as her lover—embellishing her story to write themselves into it—that the owner of the Diamond's Club was the heiress of a wealthy Wall Street banker, that at a college ball, Edith fell madly in love with her dancer, a young Italian architect, as mortally handsome as he was divinely impecunious. She allowed herself to be spirited away to marry her flirt on board a passenger ship that brought them to Europe. Or that during the war, her husband enrolled in the air force in the Trentin aviation, and the young woman had followed him to the front in the American Red Cross. That one day, two aviators were brought to the lazaret, who both arrived at the same time, her husband and his adversary, a certain German Baron, that her husband was all but dead and that due to the care and devotion of Edith, she succeeded in bringing the Baron back from the brink of death. During his recovery, he had fallen madly in love with his nurse. Edith had married him after the war, and then was ruined by inflation; the couple (according to this account, it was a faux ménage, and Edith had never been married) came to Rio to live. They moved to Rio, where they often were seen together in the Copacabana casino.

Then, one day, Baron von Kleinmichel disappeared. The mysterious American had opened the Diamond's Club, where she was a sensation, living under the assumed name Edith de Berensdorff. She drank, danced, played the femme fatale, provoked men, led them on without being seduced by any of them, and left no room for a rumour linking her to any man's name. On the other hand, it was said that she had an extraordinary artistic ability to allow herself to be given gifts and an insatiable passion for diamonds. More than a few Brill-creamed and perfumed dandies had vainly claimed to have already offered her two or three diamonds.

As far as I could see, of all her admirers, my friend Luiz came the closest to this enigmatic woman. Luiz saw this American for what she was—a spoiled brat like the other Broadway girls. He had visited her twice, as a gentleman, with honour. They drank copiously and in style, and Edith tried to persuade him to take her to a jeweller on the rua Ovidor the second time. She had chosen a magnificent blue diamond that Luiz had paid for by executing numerous bank drafts—and I can promise you that Luiz d'Aranha was not a *coquebin* sucker, quite the contrary. He had dealt with dancers by the dozen, this Brazilian seducer, in London, Paris, Berlin, Amsterdam, and Chicago when he travelled pre-crisis for his international tapioca business.

The first time I encountered the Diamond's Club owner, I was, and I had been warned, absolutely dazzled by the grace and luminous beauty of a femme fatale born to the role. But it didn't take me long to conclude that Edith de Bernesdorff was pushing beyond her limits and that each night, just as she allowed herself to be spirited into the constant whirlpool of dances that were practiced in her club—and Edith threw herself into them all, either of the South or of the North. At her table, surrounded by a circle of her admirers who were dying of jealousy, she laughed, titillated, and provoked. Capricious or tenderly familiar, she still acted like an automaton in my eyes.

In her boisterous club, she was the schemer-in-chief, the larger-than-life character, the instigator. I often had the impression that the owner of the Diamond's Club was the only person unaware of its goings-on. Even when, like a professional courtesan, she pulled her dancer against her or raised her champagne to the lips of a sentimental bird, bleached with emotion but flushed with cash, I observed that she was in a torpor, semi-conscious.

I concluded that this American woman was a seriously neurotic head-case, a certifiable madwoman, or at the very least, barmy. But I had never heard that Edith de Berensdorff took drugs; otherwise, the heavyweights of Rio de Janeiro would not have tolerated the Diamond's Club, a wild dance club that was unrivalled.

* * *

One of those nights, when things were hitting their usual delirious tempo, Edith suddenly shrieked out: "Otto! ... Otto! ... Look out! He's going to kill you!"

Pivoting, she fell onto the waxed floor, her two hands clutching her heart. The exquisite creature whimpered: "Aie! I'm dying!"

And, before passing out, squirming on the ground, she murmured again, two or three times the name "Otto." Then lapsed into unconsciousness.

Luiz and I were the first to rush towards her, and having summoned a car, we immediately transported Edith to her home.

When she eventually revived, we had a lot of trouble trying to make out what she was saying. She spoke in a raw, garbled gasp, unable to articulate all the words distinctly or even finish her phrases:

"Ah! Men! ... They're like children. They think that ... I told Otto that he wouldn't survive. If he loved me, he never would have left ... he knew, poor darling! During that time in Rio, I was collecting diamonds ... I had as many as I wanted. I hid them in a bag ... But men, they never understand anything, no, never ... You could see me nude, dance nude, but nobody has ever seen me wear my jewels ... They were for him, all of them, all, all ... Ah! If only he had listened to me ... poor boy! ... I told him he'd come back flat broke ... And, now, they've killed him ... Oh!"

We arrived at her home and laid her out on her bed. While digging around the bathroom, Luiz took her clothes off, looking for salts, a flask of eau-de-Cologne, a clean towel, linen, a bathrobe and pyjamas. Having opened the drawer of her dressing table, I put my hand on a leather pocket, similar to what trappers carry when they go into the forest and usually used for their smoking *impedimenta* such as lighters and matches; it was made out of muskrat skin and watertight. Edith's pocket was filled with diamonds in bulk. It showcased every possible colour and every size and displayed the names of the most prestigious jewellers in Rio. It overflowed out of the jumble of the small drawer.

Thus, in panic, this girl was spilling out the truth, disclosing her innermost secret. She never thought of anything but the man she adored and her great disillusion when the baron returned, like so many other seekers returning from the depths of the jungle, empty-handed and miserable from the hell of *Rio das Garças*.

And now she revealed that he'd been shot to death, and she sobbed ...

Poor Edith! I left her in my friend's good care. I returned alone to the hotel. As the taxi raced down the length of the still-deserted beach at dawn, I wondered about this unexpected scene in the Diamond's Club that night. Had I witnessed the theatre of a hysterical crisis, which had struck a woman senseless and on the verge of a nervous breakdown? Or had I just witnessed an extreme case of telepathy?

III

I have asked myself this question many times but have only recently come to the answer. This was due to a chance encounter on the platform for Bus 19, passing in front of my door at Alma[10] in the direction of Gare de Lyon.

---

10. At the time, Cendrars resided either at the Alma-Hotel (since closed down) owned by Mme Lampen, 12 avenue Montaigne, just opposite the Comédie des Champs-Elysées, or in his "country cottage" in Tremblay-sur-Mauldre.

I had just paid my ticket to the conductor and lit a cigarette when I noticed a fellow rider. He stood like me, cigarette dangling from his mouth, and cast me a sympathetic smile.

"You don't recognize me, monsieur Cendrars?" he finally said. "But, you know me well. I was the bartender on the Parana plane, back in the depths of Brazil, when ..."

Immediately, I recognized this boy. His name escaped me, it's true, but he belonged to this type, so rare in overseas countries, of French adventurers you're always happy to meet because they are such babblers & raconteurs, jokers, at your service and yet, disinterested. They have *la manière*, an art as if their life was free of charge,[11] where the prototype is the book of *Pourquoi Pas*. Commander Charent sketched their portrait on 1 May 1904 in recounting his expedition to the South Pole:

> When I worked here in the laboratory, I was surprised by an amusing conversation between the cook and Toby, the on-board mascot. The funniest is that this pig appeared to understand and respond with growls and grunts, indeed a very expressive man. This cook is an extraordinary man; we took him on board the very morning of our departure for Buenos Aires, without any verification or reference. We don't even know whether the name he gave us was his, and he never agreed to tell us his age. To hear it from his side, he had seen and read everything, and if we took him at his word, he could be everywhere at once. He certainly was well-educated

---

11. Cendrars is mixing up the expedition of the *Pourquoi pas?* (1908–1910) with that of the *Français* (1903–1905) that this passage is an excerpt from (Jean Charcot, *Autour du Pôle Sud*, Ernest Flammarion, 1926, volume I, p. 143). He had already used the memories of Charcot to describe the sojourn of Dan Yack to the South pole in *Dan Yack* (1929). In *Voyages et aventures du capitaine Hatteras* (1866), Jules Verne portrays an English seaman haunted by the desire to be the first to reach the North pole. After tragic trials, he arrives there but goes mad.

and travelled a little everywhere while watching and observing. He was a character straight out of a novel, and we half expected to see him arrive one day and tell us that he was Captain Hatteras and that he knew the route to the pole itself. In the meantime, he performed some massive services: a *débrouillard*, a go-to man for all occasions in the supreme degree, a fantastic creator of cuisine, and a baker to boot, a worker, polite, and easy to get along with, on top of all that, a good sailor. We couldn't have fallen on anyone better; even his eccentricities had charm.

"What, is it really you?" I exclaimed. "You're coming back home or heading out?"

"I'm headed for Marseilles. Tomorrow."

"*Veinard!* Lucky man!" I exclaimed again. "But you've got a minute. Let's have a drink."

So, we got off at the next bus stop and set up quarters on the terrace of the first café we fell upon. We launched into one of those conversations that only two unrepentant globetrotters can easily engage in. During a short quarter of an hour, you do several tours of the world, asking, giving, bartering news, information, tips and inside information on every sort of thing—people, the good and the four corners of the planet, who to talk about this and that. And then, after clinking glasses, you separate with a handshake, without even thinking of exchanging names since the impression of having crossed paths is so strong. In the end, they chatter about the whole world; but what they've really done is talk about themselves.

We were no exceptions to this rule. If my friend had known my name, having seen it in *Paris-Soir*, all I could say was that this boy—judging from his accent—probably came from the Bordeaux region. I nicknamed him the "Gascon du Musée Cluny." Our conversation took place on the terrace of a café just opposite the thermal waters of Emperor Julien the Apostate.

I will only report from this conversation the passage that provided the key to this story, for which I am indebted to my unknown friend. The rest is best left unsaid.

* * *

"You know, maybe, monsieur Cendrars, that this airline that you inaugurated in 1928 went bankrupt not long after? The Brazilians love their country but aren't curious to discover it, especially the pilot and me; we went through my entire stash of cash. The Sete Quedas of Parana and the Iguassù Falls are the most beautiful show in the universe. There were only the Canadian engineers of the Light and Power who came to purchase the waterfalls for their electricity trust, a few German tourists, here and there, a fat-rich Yankee or a Scottish lord who came to fish or hunt in the region. Oh, and, of course, Lloyd George[12] in person. And another time, a Hollywood cameraman on the plane. Lloyd George was maybe a great man. Maybe it was a great honour to have him as a client. But for me, what a wanker! He could barely make his way through half a bottle of Perrier. After that, I might as well have shut down shop. I didn't have any more illusions. I lost my courage. I said to myself: 'True, it's not worth the trouble to send a great man to inspect a new country if the great man in question is such a *pussy gâteau* that he doesn't get thirsty when it's warm!' So, when after him, the cameraman who had boarded informed me that he was sticking around in the country and was going to go on his own tour, I offered my services to accompany him everywhere. He was as right as rain as you could expect such a man to be, the man with all the camera equipment, and not proud, and he had been my best client on the line. I stayed with him for nearly two years. We did Parana, Paraguay, Matto Grosso and Goyaz. We tried everything possible. A hunt for the

12. David Lloyd George—(1863–1945), British politician, Prime Minister from 1916–1922.

onça, the tiger of Brazil, fished for *boto*,[13] a fish that speaks and resembles the human face in a grotesque way. Once, we saw a gut-wrenching fight between a boa serpent and a tapir. We lost whole days monitoring birds in their nest to catch them in the act, and naturally, we landed anywhere we could spot men. We witnessed dances of savages with their women and their children, gold diggers in their trenches, and hunters of egrets and butterflies."

"Did you ever track the diamond diggers?"

"Yeah. The boss was a devilish lad. One day, in Cuyaba, he heard talk of a camp of diamond diggers in the area. We had purchased mules and went to see what was up with the plane. It was in the middle of nowhere, lost in the forests, at high altitude in the mountains. The camp wasn't easy to discover. We took fifteen days to get there. We ..."

"Tell me, did you by any chance come across the camp of the *Rio das Garças*?"

"What, you know this hellhole, monsieur Cendrars?"

"No, but I've heard about it. There are some decent stones to be found."

"Oh! Don't even talk to me about that. It is better to stay a clerk in a hardware store. The trade of diamond digger is the most disappointing one on earth. A gold digger, when he has discovered a vein, he can exploit it. He knows that he's got wealth for a long time to come. The more he digs, the more he will find gold, which gives him the gusto to get down to work in earnest. But the diamond digger, it's another deal. On the first day, he can fall on a stone as big as your fist, and that is worth a thousand and loose change, but if he gets stubborn, he might scratch away for months and months and

---

13. Boto, for bôto: Youngest of the rivers, the Bôto constitutes one of the most popular Brazilian myths. In the waters of the Amazon rivers, before the cascades, swims and reigns the Bôto, red, following the small craft transporting women [...] At dusk, he transformed into a young, elegant man, dressed in white, magnificent dancer, invincible drinker, seducers of damsels of the riverbank villages [...] He is kept at a distance by throwing garlic in the waterways [...]

pound and crush tons of *caillasse* without ever finding anything more at the same site. It's so bad that after a year, he is back to nothing and has lost his health because, you know, it's tough tracking the diamond; nobody can survive it for long. Listen, on the *Rio das Garças*, you can see diamonds glittering in the river midday. *Eh bien!* The diggers prefer driving themselves to death by working the rock, smashing it with hammers rather than plunging into the water, because of the vicious beasts, the piranhas and the *araias* that infest the river. You can also catch worms as long as your arm that will eat out your eyes. Then there are the insects who give you tumours."

"Did you stay for long?"

"Oh! You know, the time it takes to shoot a bit of film. Then we got the hell out of there. The rainy season had just started, and we wanted to get out and fast before being paralyzed by the floods."

"What year was this?"

"1930.[14]"

"And what month?"

"February, March. At the beginning of the rains."

The date was a fit. So, I started to think about Edith and this famous night of the Rio carnival, when this crazed or extra-lucid, maniacal woman had announced to us the death of her lover. Was it possible? Was I about to learn the solution to this enigma that had so intrigued me? One wonders with what anxiety I hung on to Gascon, who was looking at his watch, to ask:

"Do you mind? Just a minute more. At the *Rio das Garças,* did you, by any chance, meet Baron Kleinmichel? Otto von Kleinmichel?"

"What are you saying? Michel-Michel? No, the name doesn't ring a bell. I don't know him."

"The diggers also called him Jao dos Barros because he lived apart and didn't frequent anybody. I was told that he had spiked his business card on …

"Wait a second. I heard about that dude. Was he a diver? … And who had even found a jinxed diamond? … A German?"

---

14. This is an imaginary voyage. Cendrars' last voyage to Brazil was in 1928.

"A German, yes."

"So, he was a Baron ... Jesus wept! He wasn't lucky, the poor guy ... I didn't know him, no. He was killed just before our arrival."

"Can you tell me how he died? He was murdered?"

"No. Not exactly. You know the law of the jungle. During the night, you shouldn't get any closer than three-and-a-half steps from the debris that the diggers have arranged in piles. Otherwise, they'd shoot you dead, sure. One night, there was a bad storm, and your Kleinmichel came to the camp. According to what I heard the next day, they figured the storm had pretty well blinded him, and he must have fallen face-first onto one of the diamond piles. The guy on guard thought it was an ambush and boom. That was it. The guard was within his rights."

"All right, but you told me the German had found a fabulous diamond, no?"

"Sure, but that's another story. When we picked up the body, he clenched a blue diamond in his right fist, a diamond never seen in *Rio das Garças.*"

"And who fired the shot?"

"A formidable type. An Englishman."

"And who inherited the diamond?"

"The Englishman. His right."

"And where did he end up?"

"Him? Murdered."

"Because of the diamond?"

"Of course, because of the diamond. I told you this diamond had a curse on it."

He shrugged.

"Sorry, I have some luggage in a locker, and it's time for the train. May I take my leave?"

"Adieu et bon voyage."

"Au revoir, monsieur Cendrars, au revoir."

"Bonne chance, vous!"

CHRISTMAS IN BAHIA

I DECIDED TO stop off between two long hauls in Bahia, a sanctuary close to the heart of South American Black people. It is a city with 367 churches. I baptized it the Rome of the Blacks.

I planned to stop in the Northern capital for a dozen or so days and throw myself into my investigations. I wanted to know the truth about Lampeáo, another famous and romantic Brazilian bandit. It is said that he defends widows and orphans and only attacks the rich, particularly nouveaux riches. A sort of exotic Cartouche,[1] he is celebrated throughout Brazil for his exploits and tall tales. The undisputed king of the interior, presiding for twenty-five years like a Corsican shepherd over the sertao of Bahia, this desert with the tropical oasis and a host of mean streets, yet one of the most stupefying corners of the planet.

Since it was the midpoint of a southern hemisphere summer, I hadn't considered that I would be arriving in the port of Bahia just in time for Christmas, i.e. the least favourable time of the year to undertake a complicated investigation, since the entire city was celebrating a feast day. The whole population left off with the business

---

1. Louis Dominique Cartouche, 18th century brigand, Public Enemy No 1 of the regency.

of the day, gave themselves up to the feast right into the New Year, to the ecstasy and rejoicing, preludes for the next follies of the carnaval, where Her Majesty Mômô draws both Blacks and Whites pell-mell into the streets of both the cities and the most distant villages of this immense country.

So, when I set foot on the ground, the lower port was in jubilation —cries and screams, masks, music, processions, outdoor cooking, boutiques, wooden horses, bursts of laughter, confetti, coils, and perfume spray. In the upper town, tumbling on the little people in their Sunday digs making more of a hullabaloo in the air than the three Belgian cargos discharging their cargo of sheet metal brutally onto the docks, the belltowers and the bells were clanging frenetically. I was shell-shocked, stunned, even after I left the docks, not by excessive sunstroke, as can happen in the tropics when you're out on the street, but because in the street where I had just entered, the sun seemed to detonate like a firecracker. The road was so colourful, with its electrical lights lit up in mid-day, its festoons, flags, tapestries in the windows, contrasting façades, painted houses, and its brutal Arc de Triomphe ascending like Jacob's ladder into the raw firmament, with an unbearable, screeching blue parrot. And everywhere, rising in a dance song, the beautiful Creole canticle, at the commencement so filled with faith:

> Christ nasceù a Bahia!
> (Christ is born in Bahia!)

The stanzas list as evidence of God's blessing that due to the birth, the Child-living had shone over the city of his predilection, and the exquisite African cuisine remains a cause for the rejoicing of the Bahia Blacks today!

* * *

In Bahia, *Bahia der odos os Santos*, All Saints Bay on the ancient portolan charts, this old Portuguese harbour master of the XVIième century, the first establishment of the Whites in Brazil, that would be disputed by Portuguese, French, Spanish and the Dutch, in Bahia, overflowing with convents and missions, but which was for more than three centuries the largest slave market on the coasts of the New World and once upon a time the seat of the Inquisition in Latin America. In Bahia, there are as many churches as there are days in the year—plus one for leap years—and yet another, to be sure not to err in the calculation for the almanac or to have forgotten no saint in the calendar.

Now, in each of these churches, the Mass of the Rooster is celebrated on the date of the Nativity. The faithful crowding the manger are not so much venerating the Christ-child in the same manner as the three King Magi from the East. They are jubilant because one of the three Magi is Black, like them! The idea is that Balthazar and his grand elephant arrived from the Orient, from the kingdom of Saba, have gained paradise and opened large gates of heaven to Black Africans and their animals. As exiles of the motherland, with eyes of wonder and adoration, the Catholic Blacks and good Christians of Bahia follow this king and his symbolic float as they enter the promised land.

And, so, in the mangers of Bahia, for the cow and the donkey scene, the donkey is often a dromedary. The cow is a zebu, and a procession of domestic African and indigenous animals surround them, plus all the other savage beasts of the bush of the Ancient and the New World. In addition, alongside Saint Joseph and the Virgin Mary (Papaloï and Mamaloï) are the mythological monsters, the legendary beings, the fish charm or the bird-totem. The archaic statues resemble fetishes and bear traces of Africa's traditional arts and crafts, all leaning toward the Christ-child, who is often a Black infant, squirming in the straw in the depths of an overflowing church teeming with the faithful.

In Black Sorcery, we know that the role of Aesculapius is played prophetically by the rooster; its song, its throat-cutting, and the sprinklers of its blood are featured in the interpretation of dreams, the divination of the future, the casting of spells and in a thousand tiny daily superstitions. Its sacrifice is offered up daily. I once saw a living cock in a Bahia manger in a place normally reserved for the star of Bethlehem. In another church, a dead cock was stuck onto the star with a long arrow, and in a small chapel, a black cock was pierced by a golden sword, from which spurted, zig-zagging in a stormy sky, three lightning bolts, bearing in tar letters the name of Herod. But generally, the mangers are not so lugubrious, and, with very few exceptions, the Mass of the Cock is not a tragedy. It is a cornucopia celebrating the *joie de vivre* of living in the world, and the animals of the creation, as in the fables of Africa, hold the leading role.[2] Even amid prayers and psalms, the assistants imitate the cries of the beasts. Some of them trumpet. Others bellow, bark, yap, whistle, coo, warble out sonorous cock-a-doodle-doos, that spurt forth in all directions, while beggars sing at the end of the ceremony:

> Somos pobres peregrinos,
> Que de longe, longe vêm,
> Caminhando, sem desanso
> Até chegar onde stêm.
> Vivá, vivá, vivá
> Vivá a alegria,
> Na casa de Vossa Senhoria.
> Nós seguimos uma estrella,
> Que no céo appareceu,
> Scuu clarão nos levará
> Aonde Jesus nasceu.
> Vivá, vivá, vivá

---

2. I heard an old, decrepit Black recount to her grandchildren who were sitting in a circle, surrounding her, the following tale: "When Our Lord was born, *mes choux*, the cock started singing in the sierra:—the Christ is born! The Christ is born ... born ... born!— And where then? Asked the steer.—But in Bah-i-a! replied the cock, rearing up on his claws. But a kid goat that frolicked in the grass and reeds began to leap, and then he cried out, suddenly fleeing:—the Cock lies! The cock lies ... lies! The Holy Virgin, who caressed the Child, heard this and cursed the goat in her thoughts. And that is why goat's meat doesn't satisfy the palette." Does this not have the ring of an African fable, similar to the many I have reported in my Negro Anthology? [Note of D.C.]

Vivá a alegria,
Na casa de Vossa Senhoria
Nos vimos o Deus-Menino
Sobre umas palhas deitado
Em seu rosto se espalhava,
O seu cabello dourado.
Vivá, vivá, vivá
Vivá a alegria,
Na casa de Vossa Senhoria
E p'ra terminar a festa,
Em muita paz e harmonia,
NO tampo deste pandeiro
Lançai qualquer quantia.

Vivá, vivá, vivá
Vivá a alegria,
Na casa de Vossa Senhoria[3]

But it would take a Black Gérard de Nerval[4] to collect all these verses and to note the naïve cantilenas of adoration and such a joyful simplicity.

* * *

---

3. We are poor pilgrims/Who come from afar, far, far/Marching without stopping on the path/Until we arrive there where we are!/ (Refrain) And vive, vive, vive/Vive la joie/ In the house of our lords!

We followed a star! Who appeared in the heavens/His clarity led us there where Jesus is born/(Refrain).

We saw the Christ-Child! Who appeared in the heavens/His light led us onwards/ There where Jesus is born! (Refrain)/ We saw the Christ-Child/laying in the straw/On his face locks of /His beautiful golden mane (Refrain)/ And to end these feats/In peace and harmony/In the bottom of our pouch!/ Throw four pennies!/ (Refrain). [B.C. Note]

4. The reference is to de Nerval's "Chansons et legends du Valois", but the obsessive dialogue of Cendrars with Gérard de Nerval, who hung himself off a sewer grate in Paris, and the maxim that served as leitmotif for Cendrars throughout his life: Je suis l'autre.

In other churches, but also the clubs, in the lodges (we know the predilection of Blacks for secret associations and the masonic emblems), on Christmas feast days, they put on small plays, fairy tales, mysteries that are no longer zoological but cosmic, as they are no longer animals cast in the leading roles around the birth of the Christ-Child, but the Star, the Heavens and the Earth.

Outside the churches, these mysteries play out in bards, in the depths of far-off suburbs, or outlying vilayets, or yet again an abandoned clearing, in a distant valley, or the solitude of a savage *calanque* rocky coast or at ocean side or on a deserted beach. In the darkness of night, particularly the night, any coins handed out during the "casino" days are called pastorales; those improvised outside during the night are called "balls."

One evening, at the *Bal des Astres*, famous among the dunes, in a palm grove about twenty kilometres from Bahia, I had arrived incognito in a taxi, ordering the drivers to follow other taxis, loaded with costumed couples whom I observed leaving the city to rip into that hot night.

In the sky, a fragile, lunar crescent surrendered to the burst of the constellation of the Southern Cross. The countryside was marvellously silent. As I drove the chugger of a rattle-trap across a plantation, the fresh perfume of the sugar cane and coffee fields and the gently intoxicating fragrance of mango trees in bloom and ripening pineapples alternatively invigorated me or overwhelmed me. I was also strangely troubled by the pedestrians and the riders that the headlights of the small Ford revealed on the off-track portion of the road and that continued to trample in the cloud of dust that my vehicle was causing by passing into the lead, brandishing the branches falling on my path, launching fruits in my direction and singing a chant, or at least the first stanza and refrain that I had memorized:

> Hoje é noite de Natal,
> Ninguem se deita em colchã,
> Que nasceu o Deus Menino,
> Entre, palhinhas no chão.

Pastoras, pastores,
Louvemos, contentes,
A Jesus Menino,
Salvador das gentes[5]

All these Black people were present in increasing numbers as I approached the location of the ceremony, and everyone who went to the "Bal" wore garish rags and Oriental glitz.

* * *

O Baile dos Astros, cosmic mystery, was a simple and enchanting spectacle. The action takes place between six characters allegorically who are dangling in this natural décor of dunes and in barbaric costumes, but of an appropriate character, notwithstanding the declamatory tone and through the palm trees, riddles with varicoloured lights of hundreds and hundreds of small lanterns.

The six allegorical characters were Earth, Star, Moon, Aurora, Sun, and Flowers, and it was Earth that opened the ceremony:

A TERRA CANTANDO
Quiz hoje Deus humanar-se
Baixando do Firmamento,
Escolheu-me pr'a seu berço
Fez em mim seu nascimento.[6]

5. Today, it is Christmas night/No one sleeps in bed! Because the little Jesus is born / On earth, between two strands of straw! / (Refrain) Upright, pasteurs and pastourelles! / Let us now praise, oh, what a happy day! This / This little God! The Saviour of the World (B.C. Note)
6. Today God becomes human. / Descending from the Firmament, / He chose me for his cradle / He gave birth to me.

VOLTA
De Deus escolhido
Rui para humanal-o
Devo ser tambem
Primeeiro em louval-o.

This prologue announces a long, bitter, specious, violent, bone-headed and heated discussion, in truth, a palaver between the six protagonists who each are clamouring for the leading role he played at the time of the coming into the world of the Christ-Child and where each character, in turn, gets the better of the other, appeals to the public to testify to the importance of the part he played in the grand mystery of the humanization of god.

In this manner, Star and Earth enter the proceedings and begin to quarrel:

A ESTRELLA
Per ventura, terra insane
Quereràs luctar commigo?[7]

A TERRA
A Terra tem com brazáo
Zombar de qualquer perigo.[8]

But when Moon steps into their quarrel, Earth and Star, offended by this intrusion, turn on her and jointly chant the duettino:

Do meu braço a força
Tu conhecerás,
Prostada a meus pès,
Tu te humilháras.[9]

---

7. Perchance, insane Earth, you would engage in battle with me?
8. The Earth has a coat-of-arms / And mocks any danger
9. From my arm raised, shall you know my strength / Prostrate at my feet, shall you be humbled

To which Moon responds with tenderness:

A LUA
E'hoje o dia ditoso
Para o coraçao humano
Dia em que baizou à terra
O Rei dos Céos, soberano.[10]

These dialogued songs continue into the early dawn, intersected by braggadocio, drollery, jokes, puns, proverbs, maxims and adages, charades, actual numbers of extravagance, but also prophecies for the year, forecasts on weather and works in the fields, allusions to local personalities and events that I couldn't decipher and whose scope was impossible to figure out, but which had the audience suffocating with laughter. Finally, with the hymn to the Sun, the mystery was told on the austere and solemn note of the début, and the apotheosis of this "ball" is all at once grave, serious, religious and one of intense spiritual jubilation.

O SOL
Sol divino, omnipotenete,
Deus de suprema bondade,
Desde jáem vós protesto
Respeito, amor e amizade.[11]

APOTHEOSIA
O Sol, a Lua, a Estrella, a Terra, a Aurora e as Flôres,
    entoam am côro, sahinoo:
Baixando os Planetas
Là dos Firmamento,
A 'Trera se unem

---

10. Today is a happy day for the human heart, / The day he created the earth, our sovereign king
11. Divine sun, omnipotent,/ God of supreme goodness,/ From now on, I protest/ Respect, love and friendship.

Com doce contento,
Applaudem Jesus
No seu nascimento.[12]

It is undoubtedly easy to determine the origin of these mysteries of
the Middle Ages, imported into Brazil by Jesuit monks and fathers,
but infinitely more difficult to trace out the origins where the
Catholic religion, from the Curia to the formalism of the cult, from
the initiation of baptism or the transubstantiation in the Eucharist,
draws upon and conjoins with the ancient pagan symbols and the
enigmas of the mystic have been intimately seized, understood,
adopted, adapted by the Negro fetishists, these millions of Black slaves
transplanted by force from Africa to the New World and treated
there as beasts of burden.

This high spirituality, which is the transcendent mark of the
Negro soul, and is the source of the vitality of the African race,
appears inconceivable to the Christian who wallows in pity and
dwells on misfortune, and cannot possibly fathom the inhuman
conditions of existence, their abandonment without hope that these
miserable transplanted souls had to endure, not to mention the
moral constraints and the beatings, during their long period of slav-
ery over time and their even longer exile on land, which endures to
this day.

It is a truism that the cargo holds of the slave vessels discharged
ceaselessly the representatives of all the people of Africa on the coasts
of the Americas, and it is almost an automatism of historians to narrate that merchants privileged physical resistance over social character. What is missing from this broad brush-stroke of an anonymous
mass is that the slave class also contained highly evolved individuals, including "welders," sorcerers, doctors, tambourine men,
fetishists, sculptors, tale-tellers, poets, vociferators, conjurers, priests

---

12. The Sun, the Moon, the Star, the Earth and the Flowers/ Sing in chorus, all the planets
of the firmament in unity with sweet contentment rejoice at the birth of Jesus.

and warriors, in a word, the "songs of the king," who were sold pell-mell with the rest of the human refuse.

These few individuals dissolved in the masses of slaves distributed to the plantations, these pariahs, were stigmatized in the history books under the name of maroon Negroes. Because they didn't submit. They fled or they rebelled. They fomented mutinies among their own. In the eyes of the Christian missionaries, they exercised too great an ascendancy on the spirit of their brothers. After all, these chiefs, with the ear of their people, did not bend under the yoke, under the whip because they bore the worst tortures without raising an eyebrow and passed in the eyes of their own as miraculous beings, in no small part because this elite sought revenge. Because also—it has to be conceded—some of them committed, it is true, the worst atrocities on Whites and that others preached, recalled, narrated, initiated, secretly conspired, punished, reigned by terror and occultism. These few were isolated, foreclosed, banished, tracked, outlawed, persecuted, signalled, branded, with red-hot irons. The colonial archives have erased their tale or the infamous sobriquet of those executed ordeals in public. For having been nailed to the pillory, these alleged criminals saved their people in exile. They set an example by their sacrifice that still resonates with the Blacks of the Americas. This message allowed Blacks to escape extinction despite three centuries of oppression, reduction to physiological misery, regimes of forced labour. Despite the relentless waves of suspicion, shame, scorn, ridicule, mockery and notwithstanding the baptism imposed, the Blacks have miraculously remained attached to the poetry and the religions of Africa.

The spirit blows where it wishes, and is it not the theoretician and the founder of Aryan racism, the Count of Gobineau,[13] this

---

13. Cendrars had copied down a handwritten note an excerpt of Gobineau: "... the source from which the arts spurted forth is one foreign to civilized instincts. It is hidden within the bloodlines of the Black people. It is a beautiful crown that I shall place on the deformed head of the negro." Gobineau, *De l'inégalité des races humaines*, t.1. P. 350.

despiser of coloured races, who on the cursed head of the Negro placed the crown of Poetry?

A barra do dia
Jà vem clareando ...
Que bello Menino
Na lapa chorando! ...[14]

---

14. The break of day/ Already the light coming/ look a beautiful boy/ clinging and weeping!

THE SEWERMAN
OF LONDON

I

WHEN I WAS in the Legion[1] at the front, during the long eves preceding battle, men liked to talk about Sidi-bel-Abbès prison, especially the dregs of the hateful desperado bastards just back from the African dirty wars. The well never ran dry on details of the construction of this notorious prison, unique in the world, because it was moulded out of a single block. "The most imposing and formidable block of concrete in the universe, thicker than Gibraltar!" they would declare with thick-skulled pride while they sang the praises of their famous block of concrete: "It was we, the Legionnaires, who built that, and we did it for ourselves."

They were proud, all right. They were proud of their prison, I thought at first. But then I figured out that beneath the rot about mortar, another tale was told in code about this Sidi-bel-Abbès prison, the Legion's prison, which had its own secret.

Then there was the rest of us, *les bleus*, who had volunteered for the remainder of the war. We wore the uniform, but we knew nothing

---

1. Cendrars, born Swiss, enrolled as a foreign volunteer in the French Army. He was placed in the 3rd marching regiment of the Foreign Legion, created on September 4, 1914, and fought at the Somme, in the Vosges mountains and on the plains of Champagne, where he was grievously wounded on September 28, 1915.

of the Legion except perhaps its notorious reputation and its glory. None of us had ever set foot at Sidi-bel-Abbès for a simple reason. Although we were foreigners, from the first day, we of the "3e Déménageur" had been branded as Parisians by our marching regiment attached to the Paris regiment, and the name had stuck. From there, we were constantly called up to serve as a stop-gap and cannon fodder from Creil to Albert and from the Marne to the Somme. During the race to the North Sea, we listened stupefied to the old legionnaires talk to us about the love of their prison.

This oddball troop had their crooked stripes from having pulled them off and resown them during the misadventures of their long military careers. For all their exotic medals, we all thought they reeked of the galley slave as they spun yarns about the charismatic adventures of this troop of old brave trenchermen who came to join us in support or to supervise us with their malign look. But, over time, any of that was lost once you had endured their taste for drunken *soûlographies,* their maudlin fits of melancholy, their shattered maudlin, Saturnian demeanour, their raspy voices, their refrains and their songs, their ravaged faces, their hollow laugh, their tics, their manic behaviour, their cynicism, their braggadocio. In our incredulous eyes, it all vested these legendary soldiers, who nevertheless remained lost children with a sinister grandeur, confected of ridicule, heroism, repulsion, and desire.

It's not as if this band of desperados had to show the flip side of the coin to any soldier unlucky enough to be in this war. In less than three months, the first horrors of the war had already marked numerous adolescents with a withered thousand-yard stare far worse than the gaping wounds or scars. I had seen more than one face among my young comrades crease up like a mask to somehow absorb the intolerable, painful secret. (I only had to look into my own soul to see that my heart was no longer anything but a minuscule pile of ashes under which two or three embers smouldered and was dwindling to a mound of ash, consuming me like a mortal hourglass while causing me to writhe in pain.) That said, the arrival of these hotheads straight out of Africa, of these survivors of who knows what infernal colonial campaigns, from who knows what criminal punitive expeditions in the extreme South, who were ordered to the front, like us, and were starting to collapse and die from misery and shame in the trenches, actually was like a salve for the lot of us. Each of these damned souls, and that was clear, were morally shucked of anything except their collective pride and their solitude. It was their abominable moral of men of action, not to say henchmen or maybe disenchanted heroes who had somehow made it back, much more so than their *esprit de corps,* which they inexplicably displayed in such a brazen manner.

Then, there was the rest of us: a rabble of young hotheads, enthusiastic and not giving a shit: students, poets, painters, journalists, writers, actors, film stars, circus performers, sons of bankers, manufacturers, engineers, celebrity architects or workers: stylists, tailors, barbers, tanners, upholsterers, binders, bootjacks. Or jokers and pimps and gigolos, bellboys and busboys, café waiters and baristas, hotel employees, nightclub musicians, street pedlars, fair barkers, anarchists, socialists, revolutionaries, tenants, taxi drivers, competitive cyclists, boxers, horse-race punters, aviators, night-hawks and revellers, amateurs, dilettantes, ballroom dancers, Montmartrois, Boulevardiers, Montparnos, stand-up comics and practical jokers, even the shirkers who made up our *IIIe Régiment de marche de la légion étrangère,* the most Parisian regiment of all the regiments of the French army, and the most intellectual of all, in short, a deluxe regiment. It was a message they never failed to point out to us, contrasting our pathetic lack of spit and polish with the Prussian Guard, this élite corps with the reputation of being the German army's most chic (and drilled!).

II

Among these rogues of the old Legion, there was one who left a particularly vile impression and who, naturally, ended up being assigned to my squad. He was a scornful, vindictive, taciturn man.

His name was Arthur Griffith. An Englishman, but that particular species of hysterical Englishmen, running on a jangle of nerves, migraines, melancholic funks, repressed with intermittent glacial episodes of humour, just as sudden as they were violent. The evening of his arrival, Griffith was wobbly, unsteady, tottering. This man was sick, all right. The old legionnaire was exhausted—nothing left of him. We held the Grenouillère trench at the time, where we were stuck in water up to the waist. So, even though I didn't trust his appearance, I offered to share my dugout, hollowed out in a barrier where a good fire was going.

"Fuck off, Corporal," was his opening salvo, and he left to dig himself a separate hole at a spot that had been long abandoned because it had a lousy lookout and was buried in mud. I listened to him first toss his bag, supplies and gun, then slump to the ground, swearing and spitting out "Goddam" and "Bugger"!

The *Grenouillère* was indeed a foul corner of this earth. During the day, we were at the receiving end of navy grenades, and during the night, we were exposed to hand-to-hand combat with enemy patrols who attempted to ambush us by boat. This minuscule outpost was as far as we'd been able to push into the swamps and was our sole position established on the left bank of the Somme Canal. The communications trench exposed us to the brunt of the rows of German trenches nearby, and their spotters could pick us off at will. So, our snipers and spotters were doing their best to make it hell for them to resupply and reinforce. Because we didn't have a machine gun in the free section, I had arranged for the installation of seventeen Lebel small-calibre machine guns, mounted in firing position on a chassis, without our officer's knowledge, well camouflaged in a caponier fortifying wall amongst rose bushes at the edge of a duck pond. So a man could fire off one shot, intermittently using an iron rod or a lever and at more irregular times of the day and night. The whole apparatus was perched on a gangplank, which allowed you with proper scopes to spot the extreme end of it, pushing back our forward line and the far bank, well behind enemy lines, toward Péronne. Since we were firing into the air randomly, I don't know whether this clandestine battery was causing much grief to the Germans, but its discharge just above the water, and that the guard at the caponier fired at will, often out of fear, or merely to kill time, succeeded in causing a hell of a racket. It filled the night with the echoes of such a clamour between the two river banks that scouts from the other sections, unaware of our snare, wondered what could be the origin of this mysterious engine, this unknown weapon which suddenly gave a voice to the entire sector. Although they were shitting themselves, they were also seized by a crazed, teeth-chattering optimism when they heard these vertiginous, Gregorian cacophonies rocketing out from our quarter.

That night, then, it was his turn to stand watch. I wasn't in the least convinced that this new arrival, who looked straight out of the sick bay and, on top of everything, looked frail (Griffith was a runt of a man), would function well in such a high-risk posting. I figured I'd better do a round at the caponier to see how the blighter was making out. I found my clown of a new pal nude, his bayonet in his hand, plunging it in and out of the bog. He started shouting upon sighting me.

"Goddam! Caporal, *c'est rien bath*, no? Class. Authentic. I'll bet there's a lot of eels at the bottom!"

Then there was Rossi, an unshorn carnival giant, a grizzly beast and a loudmouth who found the trenches weren't deep enough for his oversized body. On one of those bad days, he dove head-first into the nearest foxhole and refused to come out as long as we remained on the front line. Or Meyrowitz, a Yiddish poet of the *rue des Rosiers*, a sly fox who claimed he was nyctaloptic, suffering from night blindness. He'd procured a medical certificate from the regiment major exempting him from any night duties. Or Coquoz, bellboy at the Hotel Meurice, a fragile lad. Our whipping-boy. Each time we were hit hard, he pissed his pants. Alongside Goy, a foreman with Gaveau, the most dashing man of the company, joyous, alert, innovative, always singing, ceaselessly whistling throughout the day, and who truly appeared not to give a shit but who had the drawback of being a somnambulist. During nights of the full moon, he would run into no-man's-land, dance with the barbed wire, launch hand grenades in all the lakes, stare into the nocturnal astra, and make out his reflection in the night sky. He would riddle the stars with gunfire. Alongside that crew and a whole lot of other blighters who had put on just about every crazy act imaginable in front of me and who were already evacuated, dead, reformed or missing in action, I still managed to attract an unrivalled collection of phenomena—human fauna and flora—in my unit. But this bird, this bloody number who just turned up out of Africa, no, I'd never fallen across a mono-maniac comparable to our lunatic-in-chief, Griffith.

Before joining the Legion, Griffith had been a sewerman in civilian life. Back then, he was the perfect, conforming, dutiful municipal employee for the City of London. He was punctual and conscientious, or at least that's the tale he was spinning in my direction. But the day that he told me about the adventure in the Bank of England, where he had played the hero, I finally understood that there was a reason why this guy had that strange semi-deranged look.

Anybody in his shoes would have lost it completely. He was only about three-quarters gone.

III

It was in December 1914 that Griffith had refused to share my dugout and, out of the blue, started swinging that axe of his into a peat-bog. And it was during late June 1915, when we occupied the Château de Tilloloy, a cushy sector to such an extent that the most resourceful slept under the tent, that mister original came to lie down in my *gourdi,* and for once, now that we were tranquil in a healthy green pasture, he somehow found a way to die within a few days, taken off by a nasty strain of fever.

It's not as if Griffith had taken me on as a confidante because we were fast friends or even cronies. An Englishman doesn't deliver himself up that easily. And this loner was far too contemptuous.

And then, go figure, the man had a soft spot for me. Why? I'm not going to try to explain that! Maybe simply because I barely noticed his eccentricities. In any event, they didn't mean anything to me, one way or the other. Or perhaps it was because both of us had a similar inclination to take risks. Every time I left on patrol, the loathsome Griffith found a way to come along. He stuck to me like a fly perched on a 7-day-old turd, trailing along in my shadow, walking like St-Vitus. He had a gift for sensing danger but, at the same time, was always ready to push ahead.

All right. I'll admit it. I liked patrolling with him. The thing is, during patrols, we understood each other perfectly. But once we got back, the honeymoon was over. Besides, nobody got along for long with Griffith and his bloody, brutal, odious, nasty, unsavoury, offensive, and Saturnian nature. Nobody liked him. Nobody. He wasn't exactly a soul mate. As a conversationalist, he looked like somebody trying to promote mime. He insisted on remaining apart, smoking his pipe. He was hostile. He only stopped grinding his teeth for long enough to insult you. I don't think I've ever heard anyone as foul-mouthed as him. When Griffith put a Malabar bruiser stupid enough to try to give him stick on the back foot, or some slacker who wanted to play him as a mark, or when he was griping about the juice, the tobacco or taking a slug of rot-gut which he meted out like an old miser, this pestiferous, taciturn and morose man could be deafening in his perverse eloquence, his rage, his grotesque fits of pique. Not to mention the stream of invective spewing out in an uninterrupted spray or the picturesque vocabulary replete with the offensive jargon of the stalls and the stables. You had to hear the swinish expletives, the droll, inimitable half-cockney, half-Belleville accent. On the other hand, nobody is in a position to testify that he ever listened to this decrepit legionnaire coherently formulate anything resembling a complaint, nor to have seen this exhausted soldier stumble or flinch, or retreat faced with fatigue duty, or have some blackout. During the entire winter that he spent with us, his health remained as poor as the day of his arrival. Yet this teetering wreck of flotsam did not even consider reporting himself ill. Especially not when, sensing that his days were coming to an end, one evening, he slid into my *gourbi*,[2] saying to me:

"How about I take your place, eh caporal? I'll lie down. Nice quarters, if you don't mind me saying, old man. You're only missing a few flowers. Don't spit out a damn word to anybody, *capiche*? I'm done. I'm going down, and I want everybody to fuck off and leave me in peace. That clear enough for you?"

IV

At Tilloloy, since the sector was calm, we remained for fifteen or twenty days. We never heard the sound of gunfire and very rarely that of a cannon or howitzers, which were directing their fury on Beuvraignes to the right around mid-day. Opposite us, we couldn't see the Krauts, who were somewhere in front of Roey on an immense field gone to seed. The sector had been prepared in advance, with deep shelter rows and trenches. There had been unusual progress. Everything had been planned. Everything had been built, mounted, and installed, and even the resupplies had arrived on the first line for us on the backs of donkeys! There remained nothing more for us to do.

Indeed, everybody was living *la dolce vita* in Tilloloy. And the men who weren't tinkering on fuses and cartridges of missiles to transform them into souvenirs (rings, charms, penholders, paperweights, planters, etc. in aluminum and copper of various sorts), or those not absorbed by their romantic correspondence, played cards the whole day, getting some shut-eye and fattening up. Griffith could, therefore, remain prone in my tent without anyone being in the least concerned with him or even noticing his absence. The new troops who arrived recently were helpful in ensuring the service. Even the two sentries I had posted there were just for show. The sector had been calm for months, and this region within the boundaries of

2. Hovel.

Oise and Marne, referred to as the fulcrum of the front by the newspapers, was essentially the eye of the hurricane. Nothing ever happened there.

I have already mentioned that men slept in tents in Tilloloy. Others spent the night outdoors under the stars, under the foliage of the wooded area. As for me, I had set up my *gourbi*³ under a red beech tree whose branches boughed to the ground in the middle of a stretch of wild grass in front of the castle. There were still many exquisite trees in this massive, devastated woodland. But the castle had been razed to the ground. It had been burned down the previous summer. And now it was summer again, and it was great to be alive. The days were splendid.

I recall Tilloloy as a happy sojourn, an oasis. For the first time since the outbreak of the war, I had opened a book. I read Cyrano de Bergerac's *The Other World*, an imaginary voyage to regions of the moon, the sun, and the kingdom of birds.⁴ I salvaged this rare collector's vintage edition from a house flattened by a missile in Quesnoy. Since November, I had lugged this book everywhere.

And what an astounding read it was. A read that obliterated time, decanting vertiginous space without suspending breath or ravishing the reader's life. You are abducted on a flying carpet. The Quesnay magical cap of Fortunatus⁵ sits perched upon your head. You feel invisible, absent, yet simultaneously present, even there, feverish, this book in your hand, that you devour, that you disrobe with your eyes, just as in a trick of white magic, to feed the soul.

Reading is, in fact, a magical operation of the conscious mind. It reveals one of man's most misunderstood faculties and vests within him a great power: the faculty of bilocation and the power to isolate oneself, to abstract, to exit from one's own life without losing contact with life, in short, to commune with everything, even when despair has fragmented belief in anything.

---

3. Rudimentary North African hut.
4. Savinien Cyrano de Bergerac (1619–1655), libertine writer.
5. Character of a XVth century German legend, in possession of a bottomless purse, that brought him nothing but misfortune.

My sole evidence for this is what occurred in this fragile, temporary shelter of boughs at ongoing risk of being swept away from one moment to the next by the machine of war. And in this infinite fragility sits a man who reads without appearing to dread the onset of what is certain to come. He is silent. Absent. Elsewhere. A second man close by is dying. A final agony is dragging him, driving him mad, but nevertheless he has succeeded in seizing this moment to engage with the live-wire spirit of the vagabond, the lucid spirit of his companion.

Dusk rendered further reading impossible, even to light a pathetic, minuscule candle or lighter was prohibited, due to the proximity of the enemy. The habit of sleep was a thing of the distant past. Griffith on the other hand, would descend into a chasm of his own in the shadows to fend off sleep from one moment to the next. It was during this time, that he would unfathomably speak of his own life, as from a distance. I had the impression not of having closed my book but having opened another, more sonorous than the book I had devoured with my eyes during the day. That probably explains the emotion I felt when hearing these lyrical words I followed in the darkness, which has remained embedded in the mind's eye.

Thus, this narrative appears to me today as a storyline, just as so many other stories which have never actually been lived, but rather as a true confession. And still, the place, the moment, the action of this real episode means that I no longer harbour any doubt about its veracity, having heard the final rambling testament of this walking dead man. Each time that he reached for his lighter to reignite his pipe, I could detect his eyelids retreat. They had a hard texture, as if made of untanned leather. His dilated eye, increasingly fixated, reflected the glimmer of my cigarette each time I leaned upon him to force him to drink or to take his pulse.

During this séance of the fading day, and each night up until the end, we never stopped smoking, Griffith and me—him, his pipe, me my cigarettes—as if using a secret code, sending up luminous signals into the night.

V

There was no pathos in Griffith's tale. What was unsettling was his snigger, which infused his tale with a hollowness, that reverberated like a curse.

"Listen up," he told me, "life isn't a conspiracy. It's one of these con-games you were never meant to understand. It's like the pinball machines and *farceuses mécaniques* in the bistros. The more you insert your money into it, the less you get. It'll cough up a handful of chips every once in a while, so you order a drink, something real stiff, and do a round on the house. You're a god! Everybody's laughing in your face and cheering, 'Go, man, go!' But guess what! If you keep sticking it into that fucking machine, you're doomed. Maybe it's pre-ordained. You're done and dusted, and still, still you're trying to empty your pockets—nothing to be done. And to top all that off, lady luck has got you by the short and curlies. You're done. A mark! A sucker."

Since he was feverish and hovered at the very edge of reason, appearing to be ruminating on something beyond his words, I can't reproduce *in extenso* all the speeches he spewed out in my direction, night after night, throughout that endless week of agony, nor give any idea of the shambolic pathways his brain veered down when this impulse took hold of him. So, I'll attempt to summarize Griffith's adventure at the Bank of England in its barest bones.

After all these years, what still got under his skin, and that he couldn't make any sense of, was that the newly appointed Lord Governor hadn't received him forthwith the first time Griffith showed up at the Bank. Upon arrival, he came close to being turfed out by security—shown up without even asking for cash in advance or keeping the discovery to himself, and had come when he could have blown the whole bank himself.

It all happened before the war. Griffith was thirty-five at the time. When he told me his tale, he was fifty. But, by that time, he was already just as mulish as the man I was stuck with. And, since he had his lunatic idea that he could only trust the Governor to fix this business, he kept returning there for weeks and months, put up with all sorts of snubs, schemed, intrigued, insisted, was expelled *manu militari*, given the bum's rush. But still, he returned, again and again, relentlessly, inexorably, even if he was passed off as a crackpot before obtaining a hearing with His Excellency, Lord So and So.

Griffith claimed that he had calculated his coup well in advance and that he never allowed himself to get wound up over the fact that he held a secret of State. This secret was his big chance. A governor of the Bank of England couldn't be that stupid. He couldn't indefinitely refuse the hearing he had solicited so obsessively. In the end, weren't they colleagues? Both of them were civil servants. They both dealt with rats. He could consult the civil register. He was on the register. Aware of his work, he had chartered the underground channels, ducts, and waters for fifteen years. He was a sewerman of the City of London. They'd assigned him to the most antiquated sector, the most complicated, the most difficult to access, the most unsanitary, but also the most important of the city network because his position was the collector of the city.

His sector was a labyrinth of damnation. You could lose yourself in the maze of cul-de-sacs, the subterranean corridors leading nowhere, the obsolescent shafts and ducts, tunnels in disuse, galleries that dated from another age, dungeons in ruins, overflowing wells, bricked-up air-intakes, retaining walls that were impossible to climb over and that forced yet another U-turn, obscure dead-ends like the old ecclesiastical *in pace*—and when you wanted to retrace your steps, you'd lose yourself in contorted pipelines and conduits that would seem to strangle, knot up, coil up, and loop out. If you managed to get beyond that, you'd lose your way in dangerous pathways, sliding channels that wound God only knows where to places also only known to God—but he, like the mole in the mole tunnels, knew all the corners, nooks and crannies of his sector as he'd explored it in every direction possible, firstly by mere curiosity, then by a drive towards discovery, to the point that he even would visit on Sundays so he could be alone and could move around everywhere

without witnesses, which of course he recounted with his inimitable conceit.

That was at least the way he described the problem. As for his
harangue, it was served up in an incongruous triumphant volley to
the Governor of the Bank of England. A simple Sewerman's solilo-
quy in the end. Lord So and So couldn't figure out what the hell he
was trying to say within this flow of his lyrical excesses, the hidden
agenda of this visitor who did not even have the bare notions of
protocol. He expressed his regret that he had relented and even given
the time of day to this minuscule shred of a man. It was all very
distressing, on top of causing an unwanted interruption to his over-
charged schedule. In short, it was time to start displaying his grow-
ing impatience. Griffith, who was monitoring the effect that his
bombastic phrases were producing, saw his opening for delivering a
nice direct jab in the direction of the noble lord.

"My Lord," he declared of a sudden, "I'd bet a week's salary that
none of your gilded flunkies, those turds who caused me so much
fuss before finally letting me come to you, would find their bearings
if they spent so much as an hour in my sewer, but, on my oath, word
of honour and all that, I would bet an annuity of your perks as
Governor that despite all your iron doors, your electrified grills, your
security locks, your alarm sirens and bells and whistles, an army of
civil servants, officials, policemen, armed soldiers in cellars and on
rooves, plus all the kit and caboodle that you want to put in a state
of defence, I am telling you that you couldn't prevent someone from
getting into the cash reserves of the Bank of England and to serve
themselves with your gold reserves. Topas là! Let's meet tomorrow
at noon."

* * *

"You'll believe me at least, Caporal? This lord, who was no idiot,
accepted my bet. And the next day, at noon sharp, when the arse-
combers, the coppers, the soldiers, guards, and the oddballs who all
worked in the place showed up, and these well-oiled types from high

finance, and that my Lord, and then he inserted the key and pushed
the door of the treasury, tell me, my friend, who then was scratching
his flaky arse dead in the middle of a mound of bullion and coin of
the realm of his Gracious Majesty. Who could have snarfed all their
dirty lucre? C'était ma pomm, my prince. They could all see, the
way you see me, except I was laughing like a hyena and them,
y m'z'yeutaient; Ah merde, alors! It wasn't a cinema. It was even more
fantastic than Fantômas! Some of them couldn't believe their eyes,
these men in suits. And others in the band who would have bumped
me off for tuppence, the bastards. But they didn't capture me. My
lord took me by the arm and led me away. We locked the two of us
inside his office. He didn't want anybody to be part of this. And
that's what I was aiming for, me. And that didn't take long. We
spoke like old friends, and right away, we agreed. I told you, he was
no idiot, the guy. I was splitting my guts. But I gave him my word
never to breathe a word. I swore it. And I've broken my vow to speak
to you about that, you know ..."

VI

Naturally, I didn't ask him any questions. But since I was also the
solitary witness to his agony, I can assure Lord So and So that even
within the delirium of the fevers, my legionnaire didn't elaborate
any further.

So, unless there's some unholy stroke of luck, nobody will ever
know by what mysterious passage, this astonishing man had succeeded in breaking inside the inner vault of the treasury of the Bank
of England as he had announced, even with the guard on high alert,
and without anybody the wiser.

That's what is most extraordinary in this story. Nobody could
figure out how this diabolical Griffith had pulled it off, and this
decrepit, pig-headed mule always refused to reveal his secret
to anybody.

Not even Lord so and so was any the wiser.

During their meeting inside the offices of the government and at a time when Lord So and So was issuing the most menacing threats and the promises of the most stomatous rewards to disclose things, Griffith solely responded:

"Boss, me, I had my stroke of luck. I only ask for a modest pension of one thousand pounds per annum. That will give me enough to travel. But why wouldn't another have the same luck as me if, by chance, he discovered the passage after me? Where I passed, another must be able to pass. I swear to you that I'll not breathe a word to anybody. My words should be sufficient. Oath of a sewerman!"

Finally, Lord So and So gave in, leaving him to exit the Bank on the express undertaking that he would never set foot on the ground in England for the remainder of his life.

And Griffith kept his word. He didn't say a word, and he died in the Legion.

VII

After the war, each time I travelled to London, I couldn't walk down the animated streets of the City without recalling this secret passage leading from the sewers to the gold of the Bank of England and, by the association of ideas and memories, all of that brought me back to the front. At the same time, I was only a *bleu* grunt among other *bleus* grunt regulars; the veterans of the old Legion who came to us from Africa liked to amaze us by speaking of the prison of Sidi-bel Abbès, of "their" extravagant prison that they were so proud of and, they whispered, had its secret.

Everybody ended up hearing about this secret in the Legion, but nobody, unless he was on execution row, can know to what degree it is true. According to what is told, it appears that when the old legionnaires who constructed the prison of Sidi-bel-Abbès "this block of cement, the most formidable of the universe, thicker than Gibraltar!" as they bragged, they allegedly hid inside it, a narrow passageway which led mysteriously to freedom.

It's the passage known as "La Belle."

These tales of Gibraltar and of the Bank of England shackled the imagination, and I found myself listening to them, probing the walls, desperate to find the entrance and, ultimately, the exit, calculating. You had to have the guts to take a chance, one last run for it, the last one to break free of these impregnable prisons.

SAINT-EXUPÉRY—
TRACKING THE
LITTLE PRINCE

A Consuelo[1]

"WHAT, YOU DON'T know Saint-Exupéry?[2] But this is somebody you have to meet, Cendrars. You'd enjoy him. He's a man's man."

"But who is he, Commander?"

"He's a paladin."

"A paladin, Commander?"

"A knight errant. You know, one of the 12 peers in Charlemagne's court. Oh! Don't get me wrong. He's not one of these aviators in the style we knew during the war. A Guynemer, for example, strolls straight into the Pantheon because his name appears on a dispatch, and suddenly, he's a celebrity, receiving all the glorious accolades of the armed forces. For some reason, they appear lost in the ranks, destined to be part of an obscure team doing all the dirty work. Local

---

1. Consuelo Suncin (1901–1979) Salvadorean painter and sculptor. Married Saint-Exupéry in 1931. During his radio interviews with Michel Manoll, Cendrars referred to Consuelo "who not only had a first name in the George Sand style, but who is a character in one of George Sand's works and the grandmother of Nohant. Nohant would have loved Consuelo, because she smoked a cigar." (*Blaise Cendrars vous parle ...*, Denoel, 1952, p. 156)

2. Antoine de Saint-Exupéry (1900–1944). In the same interview with Manoll, Cendrars said he had met Saint-Exupéry four times, "once in the café Aux Deux Magots, another time in Gide's home, a third time at the Brasserie Lipp, and a fourth time, when we were filming Courrier Sud at Paramount." He got a big kick out of his laugh.

heroes but, at the same time, unreal beings belonging to a distant, transcendental constellation. But that's not the case here. Saint-Exupéry was, above all, a very simple man, just a man. Like you and me, Cendrars, because he belongs to a new generation of aviators, hitched, like us at the time, to the front of an immense task, the creation of Air Post. And I assure you that the airline pilots are doing good work for France."

So, Saint-Exupery is a *costaud*, a beast, but then, he's also got his tender side: he's pugnacious and likes mixing it up. But there's more. He's also the most devoted and skilled guy in the Juby field. He's an ace, an enthusiast, but he's also the most cool and untroubled of the whole brood. Often, he can be the dark, taciturn one, moody enough to cast a shadow on the entire team, but then, he's also a wild man. A regular digger. The life of the party, who loves laughing and enjoying himself, yet adept at the art of doing nothing. He happens to be the craziest daredevil pilot of the line while remaining a most devoted comrade. There's no vanity in the man, you can imagine, because he adores taking the piss out of himself. In short, he's a bloody *poilu*! But at the same time, he's still a paladin, a nobleman because he's an adventurer, a knight errant, and fiercely loyal to a fault.

So, it's in these terms that, for the first time, I heard about Antoine de Saint-Exupéry. It was in 1929, on board the Noirmoutier,[3] a cargo of the *Compagnie des Armateurs Français Réunis*. I was returning to France after a sojourn in Brazil. While boarding at Pernambouc, where we had a stopover, I was surprised and thrilled to meet among the scattered passengers on the steamboat Commander Deloeil,[4] an

---

3. *Le Noirmoutier* replaced *Le Croix* in the drafts, and, in place of the *Compagnie des Chargeurs Réunis*, is substituted the *Compagnie des Armateurs Français Réunis*. R. Guyon notes that this latter company never existed and that the *Noirmoutier*, just as is the case with the *Ile-de-Ré* (see supra note 4) is not registered with any boat of the time when Cendrars wrote his piece. His final return from Brazil was in 1928 (and not in 1929) on the Lutetia. Why this substitution? Perhaps because at Noirmoutier "Blackmonastery," boarding point for the convicts of Guyane, was a locality called Port-des-Cendres" (Echos du bastingage [Echoes of the Bulwark], op.cit. pl. 119).
4. The reappearance of Commander Deloeil, already encountered in *Le Rayon Vert*, contributes to make of the tale a "true tale," testified by the life of the author.

old artillery officer whom I knew on the front but without knowing him, one night in Champagne since he was positioning his batteries, and camouflaged his weapons in a patch of fir trees in the small forest of Brosse-à-Dents. At the head of my squadron, I had taken advantage of the occasion to swipe a barrel of plonk from the gunners. So, the Commander and I were crossing paths for the second time in several years in mid-Atlantic, and before long, we were at the bar, knocking back drinks and trading lies like the two old cronies that we were.

We were talking aviation, the conquest of space, the transformation that the major airlines of the 20th century would bring, not in the way the railways had changed things in the 19th century, i.e. the external appearance of the globe, but of the intimate knowledge that men would have of the planet Earth, and that is used by men as a sort of existential cockpit to drive their interpretation of what lay in the outside world.

After a long chin-wag on dates and names—Blériot, Garros, Lindbergh—I had been telling the commander about the death of Latham in the Sudan, killed during a hunt by a buffalo that had charged him—Commander Deloeil began eulogizing on Saint-Exupéry with a handful of his anecdotes.

* * *

The Commander had no shortage of anecdotes on Saint-Exupéry. Since that evening, I've heard quite a few more from others: how Saint-Exupéry believed one night that he had contracted leprosy, how Saint-Exupéry found himself flying into a headwind, the famous *pampero*, which was gusting at 100 metres per second. That adds up to 360 kilometres per hour, more or less the speed of a plane breaking the sound barrier. He felt like he was being held immobile in an armchair suspended between the heavens and earth and began meditating on the philosophy of Aristotle and Plato. How Saint-Exupéry, receiving a seaplane in Saint-Raphael, carried out an underwater exploration that enchanted him but that almost cost him his life. Among all these anecdotes, I only want to repeat one because it shows the reckless daredevil side, i.e. the purest aspect of a hero—and the real adventures to which a poet and airline pilot is exposed daily.

* * *

In December 1927, several months before the Moors of the Rio de Oro captured Reine and Serre, Commander Deloeil described the life and times of the old hands in Dakar, particularly the Aéropostale pilots. The airspace of Spanish Mauritania was deemed so dangerous that mail had to leave with an escort.

One fine morning, two planes left Saint-Louis-de-Sénégal. In one, Guillaumet and Saint-Exupéry transported the mail. In the other, Maurice Dumesnil, flying alone, was the escort. Before Port-Etienne, the motor of the first plane stalled, the propeller slowed to a stop, and the aircraft descended to an emergency landing, jolting and careening into the bush.

For an hour, Dumesnil circled above the crashed plane. He spotted his buddies exiting from their cabin. So, he started to forage in the tangled bush for an open field where he could land, take the mail and continue the mission. Finally, he spotted a pair of them on a strip of land, almost free of obstacles. The letter T appeared on the ground, signalling the wind-path.

He landed as close to them as possible without crashing, and immediately, the three aviators shifted the mail as if it were the holy grail.

But since Dumesnil's plane, an old Bréguet, was incapable of transporting all three pilots at once, they decided that Guillaumet, who was ill and exhausted by fever, would set out on his own and send out a party to save his friends right after getting the mails safely delivered to Port-Etienne.

Saint-Exupéry and Dumesnil turned the plane into the wind, and Buillaumet lifted off. The two others watched him disappear, suddenly plunging into the dunes and disappearing into a valley. Dead worried and fearing the worst, Saint-Exupéry and Dumesnil raced towards the scene.

They ran until exhaustion slowed them down. One carried the drug box, the other the food supply. They walked straight ahead. The sun was scalding, and they were dying of thirst. They buried themselves in the burning sand, spotted an oxbow lake, and waded through the waist-high, fetid water. They were utterly isolated. At intervals, they fired off revolver shots to warn Guillaumet of their proximity, as they feared he was wounded or worse. In this way, they walked for seven hours, covering 10 kilometres. Saint-Exupéry, who suffered from arthritis, was near exhaustion and wondered how he was going to continue when suddenly, from the top of a dune, the two loyal heroes spotted the plane of their friend, who had somehow managed to make a safe landing.

Hope was rekindled.

Saint-Exupéry and Dumesnil immediately fired off their revolvers. Guillaumet didn't respond. Angst gripped them anew. Had the Moors abducted their comrade? Had he blacked out? Was he wounded? They began running again.

When they arrive at the plane, what do they see? Guillaumet stretched out under the plane, in the shade, sleeping peacefully!

They shook him awake, shouting joyfully.

"No worries!" he says. "Engine stall caused by the heat. Everything's fine."

The three men set things up and camped down. They emptied the water from the radiator and filtered it. Finally, they could drink. They had a snack. At nightfall, not giving too much thought to the proximity of the Moors that the flame might attract, they kindled a fire under a swarm of mosquitoes buzzing in a cloud above them.

What to do, though? They were sure that a backup plane would come looking for them. Certainly, but when?

So, they didn't have to respond to this annoying question or think about what the fates had visited upon them. Saint-Exupéry recalled having stuffed a chess game inside the plane's hold and proposed a game.

It was a "take no prisoner" gala that lasted three days, three days awake until the arrival of the emergency aircraft.

* * *

Return to Paris. A bookseller friend specializing in aviation history and who had provided me with information on Saint-Exupéry in the past informed me that the young man I just presumed was a pilot, end of, had just published his first book and that it was not just any book but a magnificent tale. When I asked whether he could introduce me to this new fellow writer, my bookseller informed me that the young writer-laureate was currently a night pilot on the South American line.

So, it must have been him, Saint-Exupéry, whom I saw passing once per week in the skies of Rio de Janeiro, no matter how bad the weather was, and with such regularity that, just as the residents of Koenigsberg during the passage of Emmanuel Kant would arrive at a fixed time at the university to follow his metaphysics course, the two million residents of Rio would adjust their watches when they sighted the aircraft displaying the French tricolour roundel.

That is modern poetry, poetry in action, emanating from reality and dreams, a noble formula for life—and not only good propaganda as exploited by officialdom. So, any writer today can be proud of him and envy Saint-Ex, who had the luck to ascend to the heavens daily, display the prowess of an inspired poet in the heavens, and then return as scheduled with a book in the pocket of his aviator coveralls.

* * *

We were fated to meet, Saint-Exupéry and me. I first spotted him inside the Brasserie Lipp, Boulevard Saint-Germain, perched side-saddle on a chair amongst a circle of admirers. They listened to Léon-Paul Fargue[5] narrate imaginary stories until well into the

---

5. Léon-Paul Fargue (1876–1947), French poet, author of *Tancrède* (1911) and the *Piéton de Paris* (1939). Cendrars pays him homage in a "Letter" in *Les Feuilles libres* (n° 45–46, June 1927, p. 196–197): "I like his self-assurance, twinned with timidity, his erudition, that he borrows from the Neveu de Rameau" ...

night. He listened as did the others, but he laughed louder than the rest.

Another time, I surprised him in the process of revising drafts of his second book in a café where I observed him. He was gesturing with the left hand, not as if he was orating verse, but as if swatting away the intrusion of an airplane that had unexpectedly flown across his draft.

Finally, a mutual friend introduced me to Antoine de Saint-Exupéry and his wife, a charming South American who called her great husband "Tonion." That day, I could see him smile from a close-up, just as one can surprise on-screen, in a close-up shot, the smile of a hero to whom we have become attached—and this smile was infinitely tender and infused with pathos, as is always the case when a man of action dreams.

* * *

Nothing but land! shouted Paul Morand,[6] disappointed. But I believe that the world has never been so vast, so unfathomable, so prodigiously alive, authentic, proximate, familiar, seductive, filled with endless surprises, enigmas and anecdotes now that we can circle the globe in several days, and cross oceans in a few hours of flying—without so much as a nod and a wink at the clear and present danger.

6.Paul Morand (1888–1976), French writer, author of novels and travel tales such as *Rien que la terre* (Grasset, 1927). He pays homage to Cendrars in *Monplaisir … in literature* that he qualifies as the "Tolstoy of the Transiberian" (Gallimard, 1967).

I HAVE KILLED

"I HAVE KILLED" *was published in 1918 at* la Belle Edition *on 8 November. 353 copies, chapbook in 12 colombier, 36 pages unnumbered and printed in blood-red. It is accompanied by five drawings of Mr. Fernand Léger, two in red, two in blue and on the cover in yellow and blue. Certain copies include a coquille on the cover. It's the first book illustrated by Fernand Léger (1881–1955). The poet and the painter met before the Great War, according to Miriam Cendrars, at the Section d'Or Galery la Boétie salon premiere on 10 October 1912. It was the war that brought them together. In 1934–1946, they took their distance from each other, probably due to their beliefs. Léger was a communist. Cendrars didn't like the Popular Front and was against any form of political activism. "I Have Killed" was a bombshell, shattering readers by its violence and no attempt to mitigate it. Like other prominent poets of the artistic left of the interbellum, Aragon publicly let it be known that "that guy who wrote 'I Have Killed' was glorifying war and the Great War. Cendrars didn't dose his memoir with the usual salves of patriotism, pacifism or political ideology, to imbue his tale with the "authenticity" of the testimony of a war veteran. He was pursuing another track entirely, trying to come to grips with these immense forces in their bare essence. It was the abstraction of any details on place or*

time. Just naked violence, a judgment without reason of modern war-
fare, the fascinating horror provoked within the individual by an
experience without a name. It is Graves and Remarque, but without
sentiment, without explanation, stripped to its essence.

They are coming. From every horizon. Day and night. A thousand
trains are disgorging men and equipment. When dusk falls, we cross
the deserted city on foot. In this city, there is a grand, high-rise hotel
that is square-shaped. This is G.Q.G. Automobiles. The showcase is
adorned with pennants, packaging boxes, and a rocking chair from
a bazaar. Very distinguished young men, impeccably dressed as
chauffeurs, chat and smoke. A jaundiced novel sprawled on the side-
walk, a basin and a bottle of *eau de Cologne*. Behind the hotel is a
small villa, partially concealed behind a row of trees—a white stain.
The road passes the length of a wrought-iron fence, curves and runs
the length of a wall bordering the park. We suddenly find ourselves
on a deep bed of fresh straw that buffers the woofed shuffle of the
thousands and thousands of boots marching our way. We can only
hear the rustle of arms balanced in cadence, the clatter of a bayonet,
a curb chain, or a can's thud. The breathing of one million men.
Muted pulsations. Involuntarily, their gaze is drawn upwards, and
they stare at the house, the little house of the generalissimo. A sliver
of light filters through the unhinged shutters, and a shapeless silhouette emerges within that light. It is HIM. Have mercy, O Lord, on
insomniacs like the *Grand Chef Responsable*, who brandishes his
logarithm tables like a prayer machine. A calculation of probabilities
hits him like an uppercut. Silence. It's raining. At the end of the
wall, there's no more straw. We fall in line and are once again
wading through the mud. It's the blackness of night. The marching
songs have started again.

> Catherine walks on piggy-hooves
> Her ankles all deformed
> She's knock-kneed
> With a mouldy kunt

And bad titty-rot,
Titty-rot, tit-tit-rot

We're on the path from back to front
Give us the gals
With hair on their butts
We'll see them again
When class comes back
We'll get them back
When class comes back

* * *

Soldiers, grab your gear
They don't see the crime
You'll do no time
Cuz your time's all up
You sitting duck.
Another Maghrebian slut
In the warrant officer's arms
He's pitched his tent in record time

* * *

No need to hide
Père Grognon, Père Grognon
Drop your gear
Show your slab of boudin
What is that piece of meat
Alsace, Swiss or Lorraine?[1]

---

1. In *Sky* (*Le Lotissement du Ciel*), Cendrars returns to this historical refrain that "causes you to cross the parapets of reason." While illustrating "the absurdity of war," this refrain for Cendrars constitutes "the perfect illustration of the law of the intellectual constant with respect to this force that historians do not sufficiently consider in the vicissitudes of the formation of Europe: the permanence of language. Cendrars borrowed his law of the

* * *

Pan, pan l'Arbi
The jackals are all here

* * *

It was a Spring evening
In the extreme south
An entire column on the march

* * *

That an African bat up in the sky
Comin by and going by
Where the hell did the Tonkinese go?
Heads up their arses, to and fro

* * *

On the left, on the right, nothing advances. Trucks lumber, sometimes advancing by fits and jolting starts. Columns, masses of men
trembling. The tremor of an earthquake. The odour of the burnt-
out remains of a horse's croup, the motorcycle pannier bags, phenol
and anise. A feeling like you'd swallowed gum; the air is so heavy.
The night is asphyxiating, the fields stricken with the stench of the
plague—the breath of Père Pinard[2] poisoning nature. Long live

---

intellectual constant from his hero, Rémy de Gourmont. Gourmont disassociates, firstly,
the intellectual faculty that he compares to a sponge and that remains at a constant level
over the ages and on the other hand, the extreme variation of its content (*Promenades
philosophique*, 2nd series, Mercure de France 108). Thus, neither poetry nor art know
progress or decline, rather just an evolution. Cendrars frequently invokes this "law" to
emphasize the permanence of language or the "principle of utility," invoked by Gourmont
in support of his evolutionary theory.
2. In "Le Rayon Vert", Cendrars recounts the quarrels of legionnaires falling foul of each
other while drinking "Papa Pinard" in *A Dangerous Life*.

aramon[3] in the belly that burns like a Vermilion medal! Suddenly, a plane takes off in a groaning backfire of exhaust. Then, is swallowed up by the clouds. The moon rolls back like the eye of a shark. The poplars of the *route nationale* revolve like the spokes of a madly spinning wheel. The hills arc into a nosedive—the night yields under this eruption. The curtain has fallen. Everything bursts, cracks, and thunders simultaneously. A five-alarm fire blaze. A thousand blasts. Fires, infernos, explosions. An avalanche of cannons. Thunder. Barricades. Shelling and bombardment. In the faded glimmer of departures, you can discern—just—the profiled silhouettes of distraught, oblique men, the index of a sign, and a crazed horse. An eyelid winks. A magnesium wink. A snapshot. Poof and Woof. Everything disappears. We gaze into the phosphorescent tides of the trenches and the black holes. We shuffle into parallel lines of departure, crazed, hollowed, haggard, drenched, shattered, depleted. The long hours we wait are void and infinite. Our reply to a rain of missiles is to shiver under sheets of endless, dreary rain pinging out of a metallic, dead sky. Finally, goose bumps in the dawn chill. Devastated countryside. Frozen turf. Deadened lands. Pumice stones. Crucifying barbwire. And the wait. The wait is fathomless. Our shelter is a canopy of missiles. We hear what we called the "old grandads" coming into the train station. These are locomotives in the air, invisible trains, telescoping, crashing into us. We count the double smash of the *Rimailho* launching mechanisms for the 75.[4] The labouring grunts of the 240. The 120 beating like a bass drum. The spinning hum of the 155. The drawn-out caterwauling of the 75. An arch is opening over our heads. The sounds emerge like a copulation: male and female. Grinding. Hissing. Screeching. Neighing. It coughs, spits, trumpets, shouts, cries out and laments. Chimera of steel and mastodonts rutting. Apocalyptic mouth, an

---

3. Well-known vintage in the south of France.
4. Rimailho: Emile Rimailho, French officer (1864–1954), who perfected the 75 cannon shooting brake and created rapid fire heavy artillery equipment with hydropneumatic brake. The French army adopted it in 1905.

open pocket, from which inarticulate words plunge, titanic, like intoxicated whales. Then they link up, as if forming phrases, take on meaning, and redouble in intensity. It becomes distinguishable. You detect a particular tertiary rhythm, a special cadence, like a human accent. After a while, this terrifying noise has no more effect than the sound of a fountain. You'd think it was a cosmic stream of water; it is regular, ordered, continuous, and mathematical. Music of the spheres. Breath of the world. I can make out that an emotion is gently inflating a woman's bodice. Her torso rises and falls. It is round. Powerful. I'm reminded of Baudelaire's *La Géante.*[5] Then, a silver whistle. The colonel launches everything, his arms open. It's H hour. We depart for the attack, cigarette in the mouth. Instantly, the clicking rat-a-tat of German machine gunners is audible. The machine guns are like coffee grinders.

Bullets crackle. We advance, raising the left shoulder, the shoulder blade twisted on the face, the entire body fileted, to make a shield of oneself. Our temples are feverish, every face torn with angst. We're wired, on edge, tense. But we march ahead anyway, perfectly in line and calmly. There is no longer a single decorated officer in sight. We instinctively follow the man who has always shown the most cool under fire, often an obscure ordinary soldier. There is no longer any room for bluff. Of course, there's always an imbecile or two who shouts as he's being gunned down, *"Vive la France!"* or: "This is for my wife!" Generally, it's the most taciturn who orders and who is front of the line, followed by several hysterics. This is the group that fires up the others. The bragging and boasting has evaporated. The ass now brays. The coward crouches. The weak crumple to their knees. The thief abandons you. Some even calculate what valuables are in the other's gear. The yellow belly scuttles inside his hole. Some are playing dead. And then, there's the horde of pathetic doomed who go out and get their arses shot off without having a clue as to why or how. There are more than a few in that last category! Now, the grenades are bursting as if they are depth charges.

---

5. "La Géante" is the XIXth poem of the section "Spleen et idéal" in *Les Fleurs du mal.*

Flames and smoke surround us. A demential fear somersaults you forward into the German trenches. After a moment, we recognize each other. We organize the position overrun. The guns fire automatically. We are there, among the slain and the slaughtered. No quarter given, no escape. "Forward march! Forward march!" We don't even know where the order comes from. Now, we're marching in high grass. We see demolished cannons, *fougasse*[6] mines overturned, and missiles littered in the fields like steel poppies. Machine guns fire at you from behind. The Germans are everywhere. We have to cross heavy artillery fire. Heavy black Austrian mortar has enough firepower to wipe out an entire squadron. Limbs flying through the air. A volley of blood shoots directly into my face. Screams rip through the air. We leap across abandoned trenches. We see corpses in bunches, as foul as a cluster of rag-and-bone men. Shelled holes, filled to the brim like garbage cans. Terrines stuffed with unnameable debris: bile, flesh, clothes and shit. Then, in the corners behind the bushes lining a hollow road, there is an absurdity, pantomime hoodoo, a danse macabre of grinning death masks. The dead, stiffened by instant rigor mortis, shrink instantly into voodoo dolls and, in the minute, as if re-enacting Pompeii. The planes fly so low that we all lower our heads. Over there, there's a village to take; more death awaits. Reinforcements are coming. The bombing starts again. Finned torpedoes, trench mortars. Half an hour later, we rush forward. Twenty-six of us rush onto the position. Prestigious décor of collapsing houses and gutted barricades. Somebody clean that shit up. You there. I then claim the honour of plunging my knife into a skull. We dispatch a dozen or so and then toss a few large melinite bombs into the mix. Now, I've got my knife, and it's up to the task. This is what this immense war machine has come down to. Women dying of exhaustion in the factories. Workers scuttling and scratching to the last particles remaining in the mines. Scholars and inventors turn their minds to the art of murder. The marvellous human activity is taken as tribute. The wealth of a century of intensive work.

---

6. An underground mine.

The experience of several civilizations. On all the surfaces of the earth, one only works for oneself. The minerals come from Chili, the tin cans from Australia, and the leathers from Africa. America sends us machine tools, and China sends us manpower. The horse hauling the rolling stock is born in the pampas of Argentina. I am smoking Arab tobacco. In my haversack, I have Batavian chocolate. The hand of man and the hand of woman have manufactured, crafted, and invented everything I carry. All the races, all the climates, and all the beliefs have collaborated. The most ancient civilizations liquefied into the most modern processes. We have eviscerated the entrails of the globe and its mores. We have exploited regions that are still virgin and taught dystopian crafts to innocents. My uniforms are water, air, fire, electricity, radiography, acoustics, ballistics, mathematics, metalwork, fashion, arts, superstitions, lamps, voyages, the arts of the table, and family universal history. Steamboats cross oceans. Submarines plunge beneath. Trains roll. Lines of trucks vibrate at a furious pace. Factories explode. The mobs of the great cities flock to the cinema and grab the newspapers. In the depths of the countryside, the peasants sow and harvest. Souls pray. Surgeons operate. Financial wizards acquire wealth. Godmothers write letters. A thousand million individuals have devoted all their activity of a day, their strength, talent, science, intelligence, habits, sentiments, and heart. And now, I have the knife in my hand, my trusted *Eustache de Bonnot.*[7] "Long live humanity!" I palpate the cold truth drawn from a blade designed to decapitate. I stand for truth and justice. My youthful sporting past will be sufficient to the task. My nerves are tense, the muscles taut, ready for a leap into reality. I have survived the torpedo, the cannon, the mines, artillery fire, gas, machine guns, all the anonymous, demonic, systematic instruments of death. Blind to life, blind to us all. Now, I will survive mankind. My alter ego. An ape. Eye for an eye, tooth for a

---

7. Pocket knife with a ferrule, wooden handle or a switchblade, invented by the cutler Eustache Dubois (18th century). Cendrars refers to it as a "trench cleaner" in *La Main coupée.* (TADA 7, pp.75–76, 129)

tooth. It is the two of us now. A fistful of anger and a fistful of a knife. Without mercy. I leap on my enemy, my antagonist. I attack him with a ferocious strike. The head is almost detached. I have killed the Boche, a Kraut.[8] I was more alert and faster than him. More direct. I hit him before he got me. I'm a poet, so I have a sense of reality. I acted. I killed. Like a man who wants to survive. Whatever the cost.

Nice, 3 February 1918[9]

---

8. Revealing both the soldier and the anarchist. Between 1911–12, Jules Bonnot and his notorious gang terrorized the Paris region. One of his accomplices Raymond Collemin, inspired Raymond la Science, Cendrars' creation, who appeared as the crony of Moravagine.
9. In *La Main coupée*, Cendrars tones down the violence of this episode: "... during a mopping up operation, I killed a German who was already dead. He watched me, camouflaged behind a flak jacket, his rifle decocked. I jumped on him and hit him with a terrible blow that almost took his head off [...] then I noticed that he had already been dead since the morning and that he had the belly blown open."

IN PRAISE OF THE DANGEROUS LIFE[1]

Part I—The Story of the Werewolf

OH! COME ROUND, come round, hear the story of the werewolf.[2] I told this tale in the small prison of Tiradentes on an Easter Sunday.

He was white. 18 years old. He had worked for a long time in construction on the Sul-Mineira railway. He had laid rail and attached thousands of bolts and washers. Then, he directed teams, and finally, he was given the charge of surveillance of works on the bridge on the Rio das Velhas.

On the day of the infrastructure's inauguration, he was appointed Inspector-General of Section B, kilometre 101 at Divinopolis. He took his place in the personal car of the English chief contractor/ engineer. He wore a brand-new uniform and proudly sported a wide cap trimmed with gold, which he also took up that day.

He couldn't hold himself back when the official train entered the terminus. He leapt onto the platform before the convoy came to a stop. His rival was present in the crowd, in the first row of curious onlookers, beside the members of the Municipal Council. He rushed

---

1. The first two long paragraphs of this piece are a prose poem, which abruptly ends with the summoning of the reader to hear a true tale about a murderer.
2. Cendrars jump shifts here into a true tale.

him with a long Pernambuco knife in his hand and cut open his
carotids. He carved open his chest. He plucked out the heart. And
before the fanfare had time for a drum roll, he plunged his teeth into
the palpitating heart and swallowed it. Whole. Zim, boum and zim,
boum boum!

He allowed himself to be arrested without offering the least
resistance. His bib of a shirt was full of blood, and he lost his new
cap during the mêlée. When I questioned him about the motives
behind his actions, I already imagined some fabulous theory of atavism. After all, didn't Captain Cook speak of savages who ate the
hearts of the most courageous enemies to incorporate their virtues?

The extraordinary German adventurer Peter Kolb, in his book
Caput Bonae Spei Hodier um, Nuremberg 1719, told the story of a
grand Negro king who sliced off the virile member of the Hottentot
from whom he was seizing the throne, then devoured the sex beads
so he would confirm his status as the King of Kings, the Conqueror,
the Invulnerable in the eyes of his new subjects. One particular day,
he swallowed 171 penises and 213 testicles. Grand Tam-tams were
installed in front of the king's thatched hut, and a huge crowd was
in attendance. Everybody was pushing and shoving to have their
part in the feast: magicians and *griot* storytellers danced and
binged the whole night, then it was an orgy of sour beer. By dawn,
the old author said the royal paunch was filled while the assistants
rushed onto each other to rip off each other's testes and become
chief in turn.

When I imagine a fantastic theory of atavism, I think of luxury,
adventure, and gold mixed with sun fever, raids, and assaults in this
distant 16th century. The Portuguese troopers coupling furiously
with the Negresses and the Indians to settle the land with bastard
mamelukes,[3] and clear a small corner of the country, the immense
Brazilian forest, to dominate one's fear and become the master lion
of superstitions.

---

3 Mamelouks: for mameluco, "that is born of the union of a White with an Indian" (Mariza
Veiga, *Le Lexique brésilien de Blaise Cendrars,* Nice, Centre du XXième siècle, 1977).

My man says:

"You don't have any idea, Sir. Don't forget that I am white, of Dutch origin, and pure Protestant. I have always worked on the railways and am devoted to my work. I even ran locomotives. I never ignored the stringent instructions of my bosses, and I always observed the regulations. Not so much by routine, but rather because life is dangerous today and accidents can happen quickly. I am aware of my responsibilities. Well, you have to know how to take the curves without slowing down and cross shaking bridges at speed to avoid catastrophes, and all the regulations in the world won't be of any use to you when you're faced with that. You have to show initiative. That's what I finally understood. Automatism, as far as it goes, is fine, but don't leave your personality behind and make sure it's available at the crucial moment."

He continued:

"So, that day, when they appointed me Inspector-General of the railway, Section B, I travelled with my cap in the wagon reserved for the personnel of the grand English engineer. I had every reason to be proud of my chiefs' confidence, exemplary conduct, and career. I knew I had finally arrived. I'd made it. Then, I suddenly understood that this train led me nowhere. I would be the laughing stock of the country with my red peaked cap. I walked right away toward my rival, a skinny, little weed of a man, a punk. A wanker. A *bleu*. He'd only arrived three months before when he filled out the office printouts, a right zealot. He was driving everybody up the wall. He had been appointed Section-A's Inspector-General to create a rivalry between us as if I needed that to be stimulated. I had walked on burning coals to get this train to cross the bogs and, by my own initiative, had placed the rails on piles and had always acted as a man vis-à-vis the Company. What a humiliation! Outsider!"

The Easter evening procession stopped under the windows of the prison. Several hundred Negroes parked on the square. They were all *en chemise* and held lit candles in their hands. The old women and the little children wore masks. A group of young cow herders drove an ass, to which was attached a mannequin covered in gunpowder, fireworks, rockets and firecrackers. It was an effigy of Judas Iscariot that was being led outside the small city to be burned and then exploded. Upright on a podium covered in fur, a young hunch-backed man sang Véronique's lament. The grave voice of a tall, emaciated, anaemic and pregnant woman joined his pure, crystalline, reedy, emotional voice. A short, ventripotent Portuguese man and a Gargantuan negro evangelist accompanied these two women in their droning. After each verse, the hunchback presented the white shroud that was placed on the miserable face of Our Lord and the Blacks fell to their knees and babbled out orations and prayers. When the procession recommenced, the march and the fluttering candles traced out a fan of small mobile crosses with the bars of the window on the ceiling of the cell.

My man resumed in a muffled tone:

"Look, here's the crime weapon. Take my knife as a souvenir of your visit.[4] I've been cutting out my ration from the everyday mess tin for twenty years."

Then, after a long sigh:

"You who write for the newspapers, if you ever speak of me, tell your friends, the poets, that life is dangerous today and that when you act, you must follow it through to its proper end without complaining.[5]

"Oh! All of you, the crowds of the great cities who go to the cinema every night, watch, be careful. This tree that fills the screen is 75 metres high. Its crown plugs the sky, and its branches conceal a world of frolicking monkeys and screeching parrots. Each branch bleeds on the underside when the sun rises. That is the cry of orchids, other parasites, and sulphur flowers lighting up. Take note that at the foot of the tree, on the right-hand side, is a minuscule white

---

4. Criminals often offered to give their weapon to Cendrars: knife as in this tale, or at the end of the text, revolver as in *True Tales* where Al Jennings, "the king of the outlaws", offered to him in Hollywood his old 45 as a souvenir (TADA 8, pp 90–91).

5. This eulogy to the liberating act is found in A Night in the Forest under the patronage of Voragine, the author of *La Légende dorée* (1929, TADA 3, p. 186.)

stain. That's me, as big as a flea dressed in whites. By shackling, you will see me grow and expand in the blink of an eye and fall upon you. Fixed stare. That's me, a big version. Here is the knife of the assassin.[6] I eviscerate a box of crackers. I cut myself a slice of venison. Since then, I have cut my bread with it. I cut my books. I cut this book.[7] Have you taken the time to notice my companion fan the camp's fire? His face is black with smoke, and the Carapate stings his hands.[8] That's Santiago, the cowboy capital,[9] a Paraguayan revolutionary who took part in this famous raid of the cavalry that still commands the admiration of the student officers of Saumur."

He concluded his monologue:

"That's the tree with the ashes used to make gunpowder when we were short of it during the war." Then he took it back: "An incision, you'll see," and poured out the liturgical wine to celebrate the mass.

After two or three hours, he added: "With its gum or its resin, we cure asthma and all stomach pains." This is done during the evening, at camp, before sleeping: "Its grain is sovereign against spells. If anyone wears it on the neck or the heart, he will resist all temptations of the demon."

Three days later, he returned to the same subject and revealed to me confidentially: "If you cull the first flower of this tree, on the last Friday of the month, during an evening with no moon, and you return home without having heard the wolf howl, or the wild dog bark, by sleeping with your wife, you return her to howling virginity."

Santiago loves me, esteems me, treats me like a man, and passes me his hooked pipe because I have lost an arm during the war. He lent me his horse, gun, and lasso and taught me the handling of the

6. Discreet reference to the Eustache delivered to the "trench cleaner" in "J'ai tué".
7. "This book": allusion to the fracture that, in order to deliver up the experience of the wound, hovers in this text between two moments of writing: the prose poem and the "true tale".
8. Carapates: species of tick.
9. Capita: deformation of camista, "a man always on horseback, charged with tending the herd" (Mariza Veiga, *Le Lexique brésilien de Blaise Cendrars*, op. cit.).

bolus. But he never introduced me to his wife due to this dangerous secret. When I leave, he also gives me his knife as a souvenir, a knife which has killed 47.

"I killed my first man at 13," he recounted one day. They all go down for questions of honour. "This knife, I once drove it into a casket."

O pure philosophie!

Praia Grande, March 1926[10]

Part II — Amazon Delirium

I am in the womb, and everything is to begin once more. "Give me the seventh lash of the left eyelid, the seventh from the upper lid, starting with the lachrymal gland," says the sage from India. Contemplation. Eye of the cat. Objective. The iris of his crystalline pupil grows, then dilates, then clicks, like the revolver of a Bell-Howell.[11] We're filming! A large white fig tree falls to the ground, and the rays of the sun and a thousand branches follow it to earth and immediately take root. In a forest of scintillating, shining, hard, oval and sonorous leaves shaped like gramophone disks, the cries of wild animals mix with the nasal voice of the man who descends from the antenna concealed within creeping vines. Radiotelephony. The sky is a chessboard; the sun cubically congeals it. Check and Mate. Long live the King. The King is dead. But in the solitude, thought moves, changes position, the centre no longer holds, and shoots flames out to the periphery. I am holding a cutter. A human voice recedes the receding vibe, sending a signal too weak to make out. A minor chime lost in the depths of the world. Today, I am on the other side of the world. Is this an insect, a bird, a rattlesnake that I see circling me?

---

10. Praia Grande, 15 March 1926: this date refers to the second of the three trips of Cendrars in Brazil. Boarded in Cherbourg on 7 January 1926, he left for Fance on 6 June. The preface of John Paul Jones: "Touch it with your finger" is dated the same day but on another Brazilian beach: "Guarujà, 15 March 1926" (*Fata Morgana*, op. cit. p.35)

11. The Bell-Howell is a camera.

I am lying in wait.

I hold my breath. I am. There is an eye at each end of the scope. Everything is congested. My rifle fires. A groan. The raging bawls of the animal and a frantic run into the dense thickets of memory. There are traces of blood. There is a bit of light in the shadows. He dies at his shelter. Now, it is night. The moon rolls along the shoreline, terrified. Pan! An elephant down. A tapir. A bear, a gazelle, a peccary. Your heart. The world. A duck-billed platypus. Take your cap off. Eat, wood, smoke, camp. Take off these oversized shoes that are cutting into your feet. Lie down. Sleep. Your head will be quickly cleansed in the anthill of the celestial realm. What a beautiful trophy: a bleached skull. You'll bring it back and hang it up above a crib. We'll still manage to make it talk, but sticking a funnel in using a spring and small meticulously crafted gearing. "Give me a fulcrum and a lever to place on it, and I'll lift the world," murmured Archimedes' childlike voice. And, he murmured and could no longer find rest. I will lift you, but where shall I set you down? On a dissection table or inside a useless museum? With a clean index card. A capital letter. Ending in Z. A card in a filing cabinet. A few written words in red ink. To know who I am, consult a dictionary and all the encyclopaediae. (Don't forget the bookmarks, references, and watermarks.) Leaf through. Moisten your finger. Don't miss a single page. You'll end up reading all the books in the great nations' great libraries, and you'll end up digging yourself into a hole of your own making, just like a worm in a pulp. You'll eat it[12] because there aren't two pages with the same taste. That'll whet your appetite. You'll want to know. Know. What? The tree of Science, just like those of this forest or the fig tree where the old Indian guru rambles, has no two identical leaves. You can always try. There is no unity.[13] Equip yourself with magnifying glasses, chemical reactants, a revelation, an

---

12. Cendrars returns to this theme in *The Shattered Man*: "Eat the book, the highest operation of white magic. After, you are God. Or mad, ô Paquita!" (RADA 5, 286).
13. *L'Eubage*, written in 1917 but published in 1926, the same year as "Eloge de la vie dangereuse," has the sub-title: *Aux antipodes de l'unité.*

atlas, and a herbarium. I defy you to find two leaves with the same
or similar palms. Two blades of grass, two thoughts, two stars. Two
verbs that are synonyms. In no language of the world. There is no
absolute. There is thus no truth except the absurd life that wiggles
its donkey ears. Please wait for it, watch for it, kill it. Arm yourself
because you'll have to repeat it fast. A bullet behind the ear and the
other in the region of the heart. Without a second of hesitation.
Because of his trunk, because of its tail. Because of its terrifying belly
that crushes you. Because of its carapace, its claws, its teeth, its sting,
its fetid odour, its asphyxiating breath, its enflamed anus, its venom-
ous haustorium. Because of its hooked wings, which allow it to
suspend its head towards the ground and piss like a female vampire
on those who are passing. The crane who receives this oiled jet goes
bald—the brain ferments. The gold tarnishes. The copper rusts. The
crystal fogs. Everything is Verdigris and phosphorescent and ends up
exploding like sunspots.

MY LAST NIGHT IN HOLLYWOOD

I HAD TO depart the next morning. During this last evening, around 10 pm, some friends dropped by my hotel to drag me around to a series of cocktail parties, apparently held in my honour, at friends' homes who had yet to be introduced. It was past midnight, well past, and we had already drunk too much in the various homes of my new friends, zigzagging from the North to the South of the interminable avenues that divide Hollywood into East and West when entering a salon filled with people. However, I can't recall exactly whose home it was; I was introduced to a charming young woman correspondent with an Oklahoma newspaper and, according to those present, a writer of talent.

"So, Miss," I said, "you hail from Oklahoma? Quelle veine! What a stroke of luck! So, would you happen to have Al Jennings' address?[1]"

"Not sure. Who is Al Jennings?" asked Sonora Bagg, smiling.

"Al Jennings, the greatest man of Oklahoma!" I exclaimed.

"Hmm ... never heard of him," replied the charming young lady, allowing her surprise to show.

---

1. Al Jennings (1863–1961). Oklahoma lawyer who became leader of a gang specialized in train robberies in 1897. While serving a five-year sentence, he met O. Henry, and later worked as a consultant on Hollywood movie sets.

"*What, you don't know the terror of Indian territory, the most famous train robber, the ace of the revolver, the king of outlaws? Sentenced to life, he was pardoned by President Teddy Roosevelt, and barely out of the Ohio penitentiary, he remade his life. It's a unique case. He is apparently the champion of all hopeless causes and the most eloquent attorney of the Oklahoma bar. And a great friend of O. Henry's to boot.[2] He wrote a magnificent book about his adventures, which I have just translated and published in Paris.[3] What, you don't know him? I would have loved to have met him. For twenty years, I have been looking for his address ...*"

"*Go on,*" *interrupted this young colleague, pulling a notepad from the inside of her velvet dinner suit, putting her reporter's pen to her lips (heavily smeared in the Hollywood style of the times), staring at me with her intelligent Persian eyes.* "*Al Jennings? A train robber?*" ... *And you translated the book into French? Oh, this is very interesting ... And you say he is now a lawyer in my state?*"

"*Naturally, you are too young. You don't know him. But, please, move heaven and earth in Oklahoma, but find me the address of Al Jennings and let me know if he is still alive.*"

I was going to invite Miss Sonora Babb to the bar to speak to her at greater length about Al Jennings, this Dostoyevsky of the American penal system, when I noticed that my friends were impatient to continue our farewell tour and were signalling me to rejoin them. So, I was forced to take leave of this charming young woman, saying, "*Here, I am staying at the* Roosevelt, *Miss Babb, but I am leaving tomorrow morning. Please note my address in Paris, 12 Avenue Montaigne, and write soon. Arrivederci ...*"

In the United States, the telegraph and telephone are devices that actually work. When I returned to my hotel around five am to prepare

---

2. O. Henry, the pseudonym of Wiliam Sydney Porter (1862–1910), American novelist and Jenning's cellmate.

3. *Outlaw! (Life of an American outlaw, told by himself)*, vol.1, Grasset Ed. Paris, 1936 (note of B.C.)

my luggage, the night porter handed me a bundle of messages. Some of them had been delivered under my door, which I noticed upon entering my room.

These messages were all from Miss Babb. While I was drinking and carrying on that night with all the friends of my friends, automatically, every five minutes before my return to the hotel, telegraph and telephone had repeated the initial message which said: "I think I have found your man. Naturally, he is here in Hollywood, and he's making movies! Al Jennings will come to see you at 6 am."

At 6 am, there was a knock on the door, and Al Jennings entered, extending his hand.

He was a small man with a weathered face, short-legged and sturdy, but upright, dry, vivacious, sparkling, clear eyes, a mischievous smile, the voice resonant, warm.

We immediately got on famously and engaged in a chin-wag like the oldest of friends.

* * *

"It is a privilege to meet you, Mr. Al Jennings. I have been trying to track you down for more than twenty years. I read your book Through the Shadows with O. Henry *in 1914 while staying with friends in London and immediately wanted to translate it as I found it extra- ordinary. Then the war came, and after the war, it was time to live again. I have rolled my stone for a long time in all sorts of countries, carrying on all kinds of businesses, cinema, journalism, and, of course, books that I wrote while in hotel rooms in South America or when I had time at home in the countryside in France. Finally, since I was ill and had all kinds of problems last summer, I found a way to translate your book. Look, there it is. You don't speak French, correct? Well, I trans- lated your book as well as I could because it's magnificent. It's even one of the most formidable books that I know, not only because you tell intimate and extraordinary things about O. Henry, who is one of my favourite authors, but because you have a manner of expression that is*

so simple, so humane, so sincere that the inextricable melee of crimes and misdemeanours within which you have imprisoned your life has no need of any other justification than your simplicity, your sincerity, your heart, human, too human, fraternal ... Ah, you know, you are one hell of a man! Let me look you in the eye and shake your hand! So, you are now making movies? And I thought you were in Oklahoma terrorizing jurors! I won't hide the fact that I even went to the police to find your address because each time I came to the United States, I asked after you and this time, from New York to Los Angeles, I didn't meet a single American without talking about you, about your book, and asking how and to whom I could address my search to find you in this lost, forgotten country of Oklahoma. And to think that you are here, in Hollywood! ... And the movies, is it going well? Are you happy? But tell me, how is it possible that even your editors didn't know what had happened to you? And O. Henry, he's a chic gentleman, don't you think?"

While I bombarded him with questions, since time was short and the moment of my departure loomed, I continued to pack my luggage and Al Jennings, far from being put off by the rat-a-tat staccato of the indiscreet interviewer, replied to my opening while pumping my hand as the fine pal that he was, naturally passing me my laundry, my books, my files, newspaper clippings and piles and piles of photographs of stars.

So, this is how, while he was going from the clothes rail to my washroom, he emptied all my drawers, and I learned the sequel of his story. It began shortly after his release from prison when he established a hugely successful law practice in Oklahoma. He had earned a lot of money. He had married and, at that time, was ambitious to go into politics. But he ran into enemies going a long way back, who had drawn a mob of voters, exploiting his past as a convict against him so successfully that he had to take steps to avoid fuelling the vendetta that had already caused the most profound unhappiness of his life. His only way out was to step down as a candidate and to leave Oklahoma. So, he was thrilled to have a commitment in Hollywood as a specialist in Westerns, i.e. adviser or supervisor in all the cowboy films. That began a dozen years ago or so earlier, and he had accumulated a new fortune when, in 1935, the bank where he had deposited all his assets closed shop. So, currently, he found himself penniless and, on top of that, up against Hays's ostracism. This dictator of American cinematographic censorship personally targeted him, finding scenarios of Al Jennings too action-packed, audacious, realistic and not conventional enough.

But what struck me the most in the declaration of Al Jennings was that this old man[4], full of "go-to" but unemployed, was utterly unaware of his book's worldwide success before our chat. And still, there was not a word of recrimination or protest when I spoke to him of the exorbitant translation royalties that Grasset surely had to pay to a literary agent, a man who claimed he was the owner of the book penned by Al Jennings, but who, I learned with stupefaction, had not even retained his services!

"What can you do about it, Mr. Cendrars, this man, him? I vaguely knew 'the Flea' a long time ago in Arizona. He was already a swindler. And you tell me that he now has a literary agency in New York and even a newspaper? It doesn't surprise me that this individual didn't want to give you my address! It's because this flea knows when to jump! ..."

"But, Al Jennings, this man must have earned a lot of money with your book. Do you also know that in addition to the American edition, there is an English edition? Do you know that besides the French trans-lation, there is a Russian, Czech, and Hungarian edition? And do you know the Russians made a film about your book? This film is showing in Moscow and recently in Paris. And you haven't received anything, not a cent?"

"No, not a cent," replied Al Jennings, wistful. And he added: "When you think I was sent up the river for less than that! ... Oh well, let's not speak of this anymore. Thank you, Mr. Cendrars, for everything you have done for my book. Come to think of it, thank you for the good news you brought me today. It's very chic of you to have hunted me down everywhere. So, can an outlaw become famous with something other than a revolver and a pen in his hand? It's rather extraordinary. I never would have believed it."

---

4. Al Jennings was born in 1863.

"That reminds me, Al Jennings. May I ask you a question?"

"Shoot."

"Can I ask you, since I also was a capable shooter before my amputation, how you held your weapon? You were an ace with the revolver and have engaged in many desperate battles with sheriffs who were tracking you."

"My, my, it was like so!" exclaimed Al Jennings, bursting into laughter. Standing square in front of me, he put his two hands on the hips, pointed his two index fingers at me, and clicked the thumb and the two index fingers in my direction, making the thumb and ring fingers knock together; he fired, moving the belly slightly to the left and to the right.

Just as I was about to imitate him, the telephone rang.

"Excuse me, Al. They're coming to pick me up. The car is downstairs … I am boarding soon in San Pedro. It's time. I'm leaving. I am going back to France. I am very happy to have met you. Would you allow me?"

And we fell into each other's arms, giving each other great slaps in the back. Al Jennings murmured: "Au revoir, Mr. Blaise, thank you, again, thank you. I have met two chic gentlemen in my life: O. Henry and you."

* * *

Al Jennings had barely left, slamming the door, and I realized I hadn't even offered him a whisky! I ran down the corridor to catch him before he reached the elevator. But on the stairhead, I almost ran into him as he was returning with a large revolver in his hand.

"Al, you can't leave like this. We have to have a drink!"

"You're right. We cannot take our leave like this. Here, Mr. Blaise, take my old 45 as a souvenir of me. It's the weapon that … Well, you Take it; it's a gift[5] …

---

5. It was the second time that a murderer gave me his weapon as a testimony of friendship. The first time was a prisoner in Brazil. ("In Praise of the Dangerous Life," in this volume. Original cf. *Eloge de la vie dangereuse in Aujourd'hui* 1 vol. chez Grasset, 1931.) [Note of B.C.]

"No, Al, keep your revolver. I don't want it. I wouldn't know how to use it; besides, I don't shoot anymore."

"Well, me neither, Mr. Blaise; I can't use it anymore because my life is finished now. Keep it then as a souvenir of our meeting. For me, it's a big day."

"For me too, Al. I accept it, then. Agreed. But there's still something I want to ask you."

"What then?"

"Let's go have a drink."

There were already a lot of people downstairs at the bar. By the open window, I could see the other side of the street and a car, where they discreetly loaded my baggage. A beautiful anonymous creature was waiting to get me on board. To handle her impatience, she lit cigarette after cigarette.

I pointed out this Hollywoodian doll "100% cinema" to Al Jennings:

"Look, my good friend, this is what I wanted to ask you. There are no stories about women in your book. Couldn't you write me a true story, a story of a cowgirl, girl-outlaw, a young girl who knows how to handle a revolver? I don't know ... a comedian, a femme fatale, a victim. Miss leather skirt ... my god, there must have been one or two out on the Prairie in your time, no?"

***

To return to France, I took the **Chemin des écoliers** via Mexico, Guatemala, Honduras, the Panama Canal, and the Virgin Islands. When I arrived in Paris, my concierge gave me a stamped envelope from Hollywood that had been waiting for me for some time already. It was a word from Al Jennings, who was sending along his best wishes and the story I had longed for.

This is the story. I translated it as is. Al Jennings is not a man of letters. He is a man who has lived and who remembers. His life is a novel that is too implausible to write because, as la Bruyère says: "We don't even dream the way that he lives."

B.C.

Blood Can Junction

In 1875, Dog-Town, in the territory of New Mexico, was nothing more than an extension of the old path coming from Rat-Station, which ran East and lost itself in the desert.

What they called Dog-Town was a shack operating as a post office, a former horse stable along the abandoned Star Route, a black-smith, a large trading post/general store where you could get what-ever you needed on a ranch, and half a dozen adobe *barraca* inhabited by miserable Mexicans. They littered the outskirts pell-mell, hovels, and shanties perched on the thick mat of mosquito-plagued land in this desolate region of the wild prairie.

Towards the East, at five hundred metres from the boutique, isolated but at the edge of the path that some of the Dog-Town resi-dents pompously called Main Street, was a one-storey building. A large square board affixed to two large posts that had been posted straight but rough-hewn bore a sign in large, red letters: *Blood Can Junction*, which was the establishment's name. It was so named because this sinister, dark and intimidating building stood at the horizon line where the sun rose. It was the bar, the dance hall, the casino, and the saloon of this hitching post of this raggedy-ass town. According to the change of seasons and the ebb and flow of adven-tures and events in the Savage West, Blood Can Junction was des-tination central for desperadoes, derelicts and derangoes alike, who just showed up and held crazed, wild orgies, night and day. Human refuse holding out while they still had cash on hand.

As night fell, the clients of Blood Can Junction announced their arrival by the drumbeat trot of their horses, who slid stopped and then reared before the batwing doors to the chorus of the yee-haw-ing shouts of the cowboys. Wild-eyed cowboys, throats parched, jumping straight from the saddle onto the banging planks of the porch, by the flames and detonations tearing the night into a ripped fabric of dissonance, the stubby revolvers spitting death into the air, fired by savage boys, holding them openly and firing them into the air or at bottles while rumbling in the saloon. It was a rare night when things didn't end in a furious gunfight, usually triggered by an argument over poker between regulars of this shithole or by some long-held grudge or a long-simmering settlement of accounts between cowboys of the region. Or an atavistic rivalry or an old-world vendetta between Afghani lashkars coming through town or who had just met. In the grey filth of the dawn, you could see the ground floor open and one or two or three inert bodies being pushed out into the tumbleweed main street.

* * *

When I came into town for the first time, it was Autumn 1875, and the new proprietor of Blood Can Junction was Miss Dollie Madison, who had acceded to ownership through a recent and curious development.

Dollie was a petite blonde, scarcely eighteen years old, barely tipping the scales at a hundred pounds. Even perched on stiletto heels, she still didn't make 1.5 metres. Her waist and face were one part frail and one part gracious, and her clear eyes were as azure as the waters of a mountain lake. Her hair was a mass of rusty, golden curls, and her skin, arms, face, and hands were tender and pale.

All the cowboys of the environs were in love with Dollie. Those brazen yahoos came from a perimeter of fifty leagues around, yet not a single one of them dared approach her because Dollie had found her own way to stop them in their tracks. A former dealer at the Pharaon who slunk around the Can and with whom I was tossing back drinks at the bar set me straight during my first visit. He told me this tale in a low voice and seemed a bit nervous about the new proprietor.

"This ravishing little slut, she's one of the most gorgeous human beings you'll ever see grace this shithole. But never forget, she's honest. Be careful. She's got a soul of fire and a heart of ice."

Six or eight weeks before my arrival, Blood Can Junction still belonged to a certain Link Cawthorne. Based on my fourth-hand hearsay, this Cawthorne was a scumbag of the first order but a scumbag with killer looks. He was well over six feet tall and weighed 200 lbs. He packed a herculean physique and the shoulders of a lumberjack. His eyes were tar-black and cold; he looked through you, not at you. His hair was ebony black, long, curly, and fell right to his shoulders. His style was typical: that worn by his type of people at the time, the *bravos*, i.e., the gamblers or the killers, which amounts to the same thing. All of them were just as good at cards as firing a gun. Add a wide-rimmed fedora of the best quality, a white shirt with narrow ruches and a loosely-tied ascot, a frock coat, a vest and checkered trousers stuffed inside long supple boots and arched heels. You have got the perfect, spitting image of this type of individual, provided, of course, you don't forget the indispensable accessory for all these Prairie dogs: a large leather belt around the waist, visible under the gilet and where a holster inflated like a tool bag was hanging and banging against the thighs, the pearl grip of a magnificent revolver with silver plating visible, a six-shooter Colt 45.

How Miss Dollie Madison, such a fragile creature, managed to acquire the title deeds of such a seedy, dangerous hole as Blood Can Junction when the legitimate owner, the brutish Link Cawthorne, was a cynical assassin whose name inspired terror and whose mere presence caused men to tremble is a story whose particular circumstances are characteristic of the life and times we led in the unsettled solitudes of the savage West. It's the type of tale I'll tell you right now. One part is heroic, one part is bare-bones, and one part is drama. But ten parts short and brutal, like our life and death out on that desolate patch of land.

* * *

One evening, at the end of a dog-day afternoon of July, the coach carrying the weekly mails, carried by two lamentable nags, came to a halt in a screeching of wheels and a thick cloud of dust before the only general store in Dog Town.

Tall, emaciated and burnt by the sun, with strangely pale and deathly blue eyes, the moustache jaundiced by tobacco juice and spittle, the coachman wrapped his reins around the winch, stood up, stretched out his long arms that seemed never-ending and yawned lazily. Then he tossed the mailbag carelessly to the ground. He adjusted himself on his seat, refreshed his chew spit, settled in, laid back and contemplated the monotonous, parched Prairie stretching out to nowhere. The two nags' tails stiff as a broom, heads lowered, shanks and hooves spread, sweaty and languid, not even trying to chase the whirlwinds of vile green flies attacking their humid flanks.

After a time, a hand pulled back the leather curtains, and a head appeared in the coach's doorway.

"Goddam piece of shit devil's carcass, good-for-nothing, what the hell are you waiting for?"

"Waitin' on, you come out of the coach," replied the man without moving.

"Goddammit, you could have told me!"

The coachman didn't move so much as an inch.

"Thought never occurred to me, Sir."

"For ten fucking cents, I'd shoot you dead right this minute," snarled the furious traveller.

This time, he'd caught the coachman's attention, who now turned towards him. His pale gaze was now directed toward the man.

"Sir," he replied, "if I had ten rounds, I swear to God I'd give them to you. The doc told me the other day that I'm half dead anyways, and I don't have the guts to kill the other half. So, Sir, if you want to do the job for me, take me out. Shoot me, goddam, and then be damned.

"Link! Link!"

A gentle feminine voice called from inside the carriage.

"Link! Please, don't pick a fight with this poor man. Help me get out of here. I'm suffocating."

"Say what? What are you waiting for? Come on! Just jump out, you nitwit."

Without so much as a trace of gallantry, Link Cawthorne helped Miss Dollie Madison to jump to the ground. The young woman's eyes welled up with tears, but she didn't say a word. Cawthorne went to the rear of their wreck of a carriage and detached the ties holding the immense baggage rack.

"To hell with these damned knots."

Cawthorne was red with rage.

Reaching for a knife from his pocket, he cut the straps and, with Dollie's trunk slung over his shoulder, left in the direction of the general store for a drink.

"Poor Link," murmured Dollie to nobody, "He best is terribly weary. I've never heard him swear in my life."

After a moment's hesitation, Dollie set off after the man who had lured her into this mirage of misery.

* * *

Dolly was feeling an uneasiness transforming into an emotion she didn't recognize.

After three steps, she stopped and risked looking around. You could see the naïve disappointment in her child-like features. She had good reason for it because Dog-Town wasn't exactly what you'd call charming. That evening, it had an extra edge to its usual sinister air, with its general store for *rancheros* in front of which empty boxes and debris of packaging of all sorts were stacked and a pile of dung higher than the store itself, with its pathetically sad *barracas* spread out and more forbidding than ever in the backlight of dusk and, in the forefront right in the middle of the ruts of the trail, littered with smashed up tin cans, that still managed to trap, just above the ground, the final rays of the setting sun, a gang of filthy ragged, half-naked urchins, screaming with pleasure while pelting stones at two old goats attached by the hoof to a picket at point-blank range. The ragged goats contorted in pain, making desperate efforts to escape their persecutors and were bleating loud enough to rend your soul in two.

In vain, Dollie was looking for a clock tower or something similar that would show her the location of a church, a simple chapel, a house more austere than these bric-a-brac shacks and where a minister of the religion could celebrate a marriage ceremony. But, seeing nothing in the area which reminded her of God, not even a front wall, not even a porch, not even a poor cross traced with two strokes of the paintbrush on the door of a barn, she was seized by a vague angst and felt uncertainty and doubt in the ascendancy.

... Why didn't Link bring me directly to his ranch that he talked so much about? A grand white house, sitting in a thicket of acacias, looking over a beautiful river. Dollie fell into a reverie, back in the deep South, rug under the palm trees, the little house of her grand-mother that she had just abandoned and where she had spent her childhood and her adolescence after the death of her parents, victim of an epidemic of yellow fever ... Why did she listen to Link then? ... Sitting on the veranda, the moonlight shining down, troubled by the intoxicating atmosphere of the Virginia jasmines that bloomed in the night., she had preferred to surrender to his tender compli-ments when Link came to meet her secretly, giving her grandiose, delirious descriptions of his ranch, recounting enthusiastically tales of his horses and thousands of longhorn roaming in liberty in the pastures of the Far-West. How could she have bought into the stories told by this spinner of tall tales? She now saw that everything had been a lie. But Link had promised her that ...

A heavy sigh inflated the breast of the young girl.

... A liar, her Link? ... But he was going to bring her to the house and call a ... No, he hadn't lied to her, not her Link. It was impossible ...

Absorbed in her thoughts, Dollie Madison had not noticed that Link Cawthorne had returned and that he was now standing behind her, her handsome fiancé, and that he observed her, silent, sarcastic, and now a malevolent eye she detected for the first time. When she turned around, she felt a jolt and was seized by remorse, born of the doubt taking hold of her.

"Oh! Link!" she blurted out, blushing and confused. "I had no idea you were watching me!"

"What were you thinking about, doll?" he asked.

"Oh, Link, you've never called me that before," she said, smiling. Now flirtatious, she said, "Tell me, Link, how much do you love me?"

"I asked you what you were thinking about."

The smile faded. Dollie was tense.

"Darling, how could I not be disappointed? I was just wondering ..."

Cawthorne placed his hands on her shoulders and held his grip.

"It's not your job to ask questions. You'll get your answers right now. Follow me."

He let her go roughly, turned and walked away. Dolly was stunned, stupefied and trailed behind him, still under his spell.

They left town, and continued to walk. Their shadows, outsized by the sunrays, now curling, of dusk, seemed to walk in front of them on the road.

Dollie walked robotically.

She was in a daze, unable to think, unable even to focus. The violence of the commotion had anesthetized her. She didn't suffer. She had forgotten the harsh words. She moved forward, then stumbled into one of the ruts. A thousand confused thoughts collided and muddled her mind. Suddenly, she realized that for a long time already, her attention had been focused on Link's boots. What a jerk. The heels. No, the long starred spurs, burrowing into the dust of the road at each step, formed small grey spirals, evaporated as soon as they were formed, carried away, unknotted, untied by the fresh wind of the evening breeze arriving from the snowy climes of the mountain range, the Greenhorns, out there, all there, on the fringe of the horizon, thousands of miles distant at the other side of the Prairie.

* * *

Meanwhile, night had fallen. Link Cawthorne stopped suddenly. Miss Dollie Madison found herself in front of a tall, dark house.

The wind blew stronger. A sign suspended from two poles in front of the house creaked.

Dollie tried to read the diabolical inscription balancing over her head. She read and reread the oversized red letters swinging back and forth before her eyes. Link Cawthorne turned his back to her in the obscure night. It seemed sinister. She was no longer able to comprehend the presence that these four words were saying: At Blood Can Junction.

Off-tune dance music—one clarinet, one violin, one cornet— gusted from the bordello, accompanied by the sound of dragging feet but mixed in cadence and interrupted by a mad choir of voices, shouts, and screams.

A door opened, and the young woman was grabbed by the wrist and dragged into the saloon.

The door slammed shut behind her.

* * *

The room itself was aggressively bright. Couples turned under the lamps hanging to the lattice affixed to the ceiling. The overheated air of the dancehall was suffocating. It stank of oil, the stench of cheap perfume, sawdust, rotgut whisky, leather, wood grease, and sweat. Due to the smoke from the pipes and a steamy cloud oozing through the floorboards, it was hard to distinguish the ravaged and revolting or dazed and hyper faces of the customers or clumsy with their boots, their spurs, their oversized revolvers knocking against the thighs in counterpoint, their large bumpy hats, their garish, multi-coloured chemises, and who held these women in their arms. All the women dressed in identical, short, scintillating skirts that revealed their legs, some shapely and some contorted. Old withered hags, young pre-pubescents pushing against each other, wiggling, who made grim-aces, who swooned, emitted giggle cries, and who all had their faces painted in impudent vermillion.

The dance stopped when Cawthorne entered the room, dragging Dollie by the wrist and sending her sprawling with a shove toward the staircase leading to the upper floor.

"Good evening, one and all! I'm happy to see you wretched lot! So, amigos and friends, everybody is happy! Goddam, I am happy to be back!" shouted Link Cawthorne, the owner of Blood Can Junction.

* * *

You could have heard a pin drop.

Dollie Madison felt all eyes turn towards her.

She lifted her gaze, stiffened and returned the stares.

Cawthorne was furious and pale with anger. This silence had met him as a direct mortal challenge. For him, it was an unimaginable affront, worse than somebody unleashing a load of spit in his face in public.

"Ah! Bastards! Not a single voice to greet me ... These pricks will pay the price for that," he mused. He saw red. He could feel a shiver race up his spine.

"C'mon, get your ass up there," he growled, grabbing Dollie by the arm and taking the step of the stairwell.

At that moment, one of the girls went into a fit and started screaming in the silence, now intolerable and monstrous.

"Ah, another one, my God! ... Don't go, girl. Don't go! Don't! Ah!!!"

"Hey, clam up, honey, he'll kill you, idiot," murmured an old drunken harridan, shaking her friend and causing the ruckus.

Cawthorne turned back.

He stared into the crowd. His mouth contracted. He was in the kill zone. Beyond control, beyond his limits. No turning back. He released Dollie and took three or four steps forward. He stopped. He was looking for somebody. Now forward again, boring through the crowd. He shoved aside men and women, elbowing, kicking them out of the way. He swore. He needed a victim, a chosen victim, a sacrificial lamb, and not one of these pathetic girls who had formed a ring around the hysterical girl who had been screaming.

When he opened Blood Can Junction, Link Cawthorne established his reputation on the first night by killing Bart Rhodes, a braggart, a scoundrel in the same mould as Cawthorne. During a quarrel over a girl, he dropped him with one bullet straight to the heart. He understood that night that he had to commit a bloody burst to assert his authority. He was the boss, fucking hell! More than ever, he had to impose his will. Otherwise, the saloon was finished. So, he had to stir up a provocation by going straight through the dancers, the gamblers, the drinkers, a man, and if possible, a tough guy, and he stared down everybody in a large circle. The crowd opened up.

Finally, his gaze was returned by somebody, leaning casually against the bar, his arms placed on the support bar of the counter and looking him up and down as he neared.

Cawthorne let his hatred get the ascendancy. He knew him by reputation. It was Jim Stanton, the manager of Ranch 101, the biggest estate in Colorado.

His choice was made. He was in that zone, the kill zone, and rage was taking over. Link Cawthorne took a step towards Stanton. Then, he stopped dead in his tracks. Something new was getting in the way: fear.

The thing is this: *pardine*, like each of the spectators, Link Cawthorne knew that the man leaning against the bar, who didn't react and seemed to be thumbing his nose at him, barely concealed his contempt beneath the tip of his moustache. Stanton hit the bullseye with each shot. Jim Stanton was the fastest shot of the Prairie. He was notorious from the farmlands of Colorado right up to the Canadian border.

* * *

When Cawthorne had loosened his grip, Dollie Madison spun around, stunned, and watched him spearheading into the chaotic mob. She was among the first to understand the intense fright that caused her coward of a fiancé to lose his nerve. She kept her eyes fixed on him. She spotted the nervous tic that twisted his mouth and pulled his facial features into a mask. She watched him spring up, use his two arms to toss aside anyone getting in his way, charge like a bull, and then stop cold at one stop from the unknown. And now, she watched him extend his hand towards the man and say:

"I didn't know you, Jim Stanton, but I've heard a lot about you. It's a great honour, Sir, to receive you here."

Jim Stanton, without altering in the least his position, the arms still relaxed on the armrest, but planting his clear eyes of a shepherd into the crazed orbits of his interlocutor, responded calmly:

"Cawthorne, I would never shake the hand of an individual like you. I regret having come here to your saloon. I don't like men who cheat at cards and who debauch women."

The blood ran to his head. His regular features grimacing, Cawthorne bawled:

"Goddamit, Stanton, are you crazy? So, it's a fight you want?"

"No, it wasn't. But if you feel like you want to avenge your honour, take the trouble to pull out this beautiful revolver that I can see shining under your frock coat, and I'll blow your brains to pieces in short order."

The shoulders of Cawthorne hunched. He didn't dare confront this man. He looked away.

"Believe me, Mr Stanton, I prefer no trouble this evening. I'm weary and have returned from a long travel. But, if you ..."

"As you please, Sir," interrupted Stanton. Jim rose to his height and turned his back on his adversary to order a last whisky from the barman.

Cawthorne retreated. He strolled towards Dollie. Everybody watched, and nobody dared breathe a word as he passed. He set his hand on his revolver at the foot of the stairwell, but then he let it fall back into his holster. For a long moment, he appeared uncertain as to his next move. The silence that reigned crushed him. His shoulders sagged. Finally, he raised his eyes to Dollie. He read on the blood-drained face of the young girl, like a death mask, the expression of consuming disgust.

"C'mon you!" he said, pushing her as he forced her up the stairs.

* * *

At the higher level, Cawthorne opened a door leading to the stairwell. Dollie found herself in a small bedroom, and Cawthorne, who had entered behind her, closed and locked the door.

The room was furnished with a baby cot, an old dresser, a rocking chair and a tattered sofa. Engravings smeared with fly shit and representing music-hall dancers and nude women were pinned to the wall above the bed.

Cawthorne was about to stand in front of the dresser, swallowed a flagon of water in one swig, and examined his head in a chipped mirror hanging on the partition. He was still pale. His anger was far from being appeased. He could not forget the rude insult he had just endured. The loss of face that this cunt of a cursed cow thief had caused him.

"... He'd better watch himself, this dog. I'll have his skin, this son of a whore ..." he muttered, still grinding his teeth, and he felt his old teeth instinct of bravado coming back. Then, finally, his rage burst out and rained on Dollie, who had been silent and immobile:

"Don't just stand there, stuck like an empty bottle. And quit looking at me like that, you featherbrained hussy! You hear me! Get your goddam clothes off and get into bed."

"But Link ... Link ..." The voice of Dollie was faint, strangled by sobs. "Link ... but we're not married!"

Cawthorne burst out laughing.

"The farm!" he roared. "Huh! What damn bit of difference could that make for me, little woman? Take your clothes off, or by god, I'll tear them off for you. You think that because this second-rate cow herder thinks he can lack manners in my establishment, now you can disrespect me as well! Get a damn move on, by God, or out!"

Having spoken, Cawthorne undid his heavy belt and laid his large calibre pistol on the dresser. He walked across the room, removed his redingote frock coat and sat at the foot of the bed to pull off his boots. He heard the click of his weapon, jumped up instinctively, and Dollie pulled the trigger point-blank. His face froze into a wordless grimace. A red stain expanded rapidly and soaked the ruches of his luxurious shirt. He lifted the left hand to his chest and appeared to bat the air with the right hand, reaching for a point of support ... then he dropped like a massive slab of granite, face to the ground and dead as a doornail.

Right then, a group of customers crashed through the door and entered.

Calm, standing in the middle of the room, holding in her small hand the large revolver with the pearl grip, Dollie said:

"He lied to me, so I killed him."

That explanation was enough. No other investigation followed. The verdict was unanimous. The customers who had barged their way into the room formed a jury. They all agreed in front of the still-warm corpse of her suitor that Miss Dollie Madison had acted in legitimate "self-defence."

* * *

Dawn.

Downstairs, in the deserted room, the barman, who had acted as president of the improvised jury, now acted as an impromptu bartender. He had prepared a long row of glasses for the men who had thrown outside the body of the victim of this short tragedy. When Jim Stanton and several other regular customers of the establishment returned by the rear door, the bartender poured drinks and called out to Stanton:

"Tell us, Jim, we have a new owner at Blood Can Junction and are challenging for the run of the town. The little redhead upstairs is even faster than you. What do you say? She beat you to the punch, and you can buy a round for the house, hein? One bullet, and she sent Link Cawthorne to hell, where he belongs."

EXEATIS SED REVERTEMUR!

You depart today, but shall one day return.

I

THE SAINT-WANDRILLE[1] was suffering through a nasty gale. Caught in the storm as soon as it left le Havre, the heavy cargo was in danger of capsizing right up to the coast of the Americas, and nobody on board recalled ever having been caught in such a crossing. And now that we had been descending south towards the Equator for three days, the cargo was taking on a big wave of water at each undertow that snared the boat from the rear, raised it, braked it, caused it to rock from starboard to port as if each of these monstrous waves would twist it and send it to the bottom of the ocean.

We were off the coast of Florida at a standstill. Everybody was impatient to arrive in Havana because everybody was exhausted.

We had lost time since passing Cape Hatteras and were fed up with the heavy sea and the intense heat that was starting to affect us.

---

1. Saint-Wandrille is a reference to a saint of the Swiss Jura region who on the eve of his marriage proposed to his young spouse that they have solely a marriage of convenience, the better to serve God. An allusion to Cendrars' relationship with the actress Raymone.

II

The bell had just sounded noon.

"Oh, la-la, what a Company. It's impossible to work ..."

Verdier, the steward, was in his cabin, raging from the thunderous assault of waves, with his porthole screwed tight, and swimming in sweat, notwithstanding the two ventilators that were making his hair stand on end. Sitting bare-chested in front of his typewriter since the morning, he worked furiously, which had done little to appease his ire.

Besides, this had been the case for fifteen years when Steward Verdier was assigned to Le Havre-Vancouver, the Company's longest line. His mission was to prepare the statements, passenger and crew lists, disembarkation cards or bills of lading, and customs forms unfailingly, no small task when all the printed documents he had to complete that required formalities and unnecessary complications became increasingly labyrinthine at each stop-off of this 12,000-kilometre line. There was so much paper because the Saint-Wandrille moored in a dozen countries and at two dozen ports. Frequently, the agent had to redact his maritime report because this disordered man always got around to his task at the last possible moment. He would spend entire nights writing, scolding his people, shouting at all his underlings to put their hands on the paperwork or the files he had lost, which he suddenly had an urgent need for, and whatever anyone said, he had never seen.

Verdier was messy. He was a whinger, convinced that he was persecuted, jealous, targeted, and who, when he drank two or three cocktails at the bar, had a bad habit of griping shamelessly to passengers. Once he got started, he would recount the thousand-and-one injustices that he claimed had been visited upon him by the Company, the snubs of every kind that the back office had forced him to endure from the first day of boarding. He didn't hesitate to accuse his colleagues, who were lucky to navigate to New York rather than Vancouver. God only knows how many insider privileges and sombre intrigues had favoured their career. At the same time, poor innocent Verdier ("Yes, sir, I say things as I see them") had lost his temper since he vagabonded on this ill-fated line. He was forgotten, shamed, and mocked, but still, despite everything, doing his duty with no hope of promotion.

Invariably, his recriminations ended with his sonorous refrain: "Oh, la la! Quelle Compagnie!" which was a lament and a complaint all rolled up in one but also a form of cursing and a challenge by which this sidelined man soothed not only his ulcerated heart but more, by bravado, expressed aloud the long-repressed hatred he felt for the Company that Verdier held responsible for all his misfortunes, including that of being a cuckold, something that was the secret torment of his life and made him seethe all the more.

That morning, Verdier was even more skittish than usual. While he was looking for a missing book-keeping item, someone had broken into his cabin to play a practical joke. (For there is no secret sentiment on board a cargo ship that the members of a crew so closely bound by the tirade and the form of cloistered life that one leads during a long sea campaign doesn't come out.) The anonymous prankster had filched the photo of his wife hanging above his desk and replaced it with a colour fold-out representing fifty or so pretty girls of Hollywood in bathing suits, three-quarters nude. This malevolent hand had pinned it to the wall by multicolour tacks strategically placed in the eyes, the breasts, the buttocks, the knees, the ankle, the elbows, and the shoulders of each girl.

Ah! As far as ideas go, that was a diabolically good one and properly executed. I will be in good standing with the pals, Verdier said to himself, putting on his shirt to go to the wardroom; right after the bell, the breakfast sounded in the passageway. I will return to that after the apéro. But confound it, how do you expect me to work with this cursed chart under my eyes?

The ship's rocking knocked the files stacked on the steward's small table. Verdier lost his balance just as he had buttoned his greatcoat to go out.

III

But far from being able, as he desired, to wreak revenge on his comrades for the insult that one of them had caused him by stealing the photo of his wife, Verdier couldn't even take his apéritif that morning.

Crossing the fo'c'sle to go to the wardroom, he had been caught in a wave from the sea that pinned him to the handrail. He was clinging with all his strength to a windsock, losing his footing. Emile, the ship's boy, who also lost his footing on the deck, grabbed his arm violently, shouting:

"Commissaire, come, come quickly. The doctor you ..."

"What is the problem?" Verdier asked, shaking off tufts of hair from his eyes because his hat had flown overboard.

"It's about the Bordelais. He ..."

"He had another crisis."

"No, not this time. But the doctor said you have to come immediately.

"Oh, la la, what a Company!" Verdier thought. You can't even take the apéro! Couldn't he die, your Bordelais! I have things to do other than take care of this wine sack. Come on, come and get a hold of yourself.

Followed by the frantic ship's boy, Verdier made a half turn, pushed an iron door, and disappeared down a vertical ladder that descended to the bakery.

IV
Qui a bu, boira.

The baker of the Saint-Wandrille, Auguste Quinquembois, aka the Bordelais, was a career drunk. Having drunk, drunk and drunk, and having continued drinking despite the threats of being fired from the Company, he was no longer drunk. He was just dead. Jules. Désiré. Bien-Aimé.—the team's most joyous clown and wassailer.

He was at his post. Dead with a bottle in hand, but in front of his lit-up stove, killed by a rush of blood to the head.

Marcelin, the on-board physician, a young doctor, slightly built and awkward as a young girl, was emotionally incontinent on his first crossing. Standing in front of the corpse whose ears he had split to bleed him, he watched a thick, black stream of blood ooze out and form a pool under the duckboards of the floor. The thick red of his blood was mixing with the red leaking out of the litre bottle that the Bordelais had instinctively preserved during his fatal fall by hugging it to his heart, and whose level lowered as each swerve of the ship caused the wine to squirt out of the neck.

"So," asked the steward, entering the cabins. "So, this bastard is drunk again?"

"No, he's dead, and nothing more can be done," Marcellin pronounced, then faltered.

Unfortunately, the young ship doctor was fighting nausea. Since his departure from le Havre, he had been seasick, and every toss-and-shift had him retching. Then, there was the atrocious heat in the bakery.

"Come on, things aren't improving, *hein*? But what the hell, give yourself a shake!" Verdier said, positioning himself at the feet of the dead man. "We cannot leave him there. You, Emile, close the cover of the kneader, and you, doctor, help me; we will lay him down there; he will be more comfortable."

The ship's boy left to close the cover of the kneader, and the two officers laid down the baker, using a loaf of bread as a wedge.

"That's not all," the steward said. Tell me now how this happened."

"I found him on the ground," the ship's boy said. "I had come to seek out the Bordelais to see whether I couldn't talk him out of some clafoutis. There had been some for the passengers today, and the Bordelais had promised me some because I had given him a hand when he came on deck, three sheets to the wind. He was utterly soused and hadn't sobered up since le Havre. He was singing, but at least he was doing his work. He was always making a racket with his heckling; he was stuffed but stubborn enough to keep in front of the oven, and since he was up against that hellish fire, he had one of these thirsts that meant he couldn't stop drinking. I've never seen him like this. You couldn't even talk to him. When I came in earlier, I watched him fall. I thought that it was the ship pitching that had thrown him to the ground. First, I called. But since he didn't laugh, and he wasn't talking and didn't move anymore, and his face was black, I had a fright, and I ran out to find the doctor. After, I ..."

"Useless to warn the Captain," Verdier said. "The old man doesn't like being disturbed when he's eating. I'll give him my report this evening. Oh la la, what a Company. But tell me, doctor, if I had my report to do, you have your autopsy. It's the regulation. So, for starters, you're out of luck. As if the terrible weather weren't bad enough. What a Company! What rotten luck! Can you believe that the front office will bother us with this kind of story in the report? Indeed, we're jinxed!"

And addressing the ship's boy.

"You, Emile, it's fine, you can go. The doctor and I have some work, but keep your mouth shut. Send me the bosun and tell him to bring the coffin and the toolbox."

"The big coffin?"

"Yes, he knows which one. Tell him also not to forget a pair of new sheets because he was one of the brothers, this poor old guy. Tell him that I'll sign a certificate later."

V

On each ship of the merchant marine, a long-courier with mixed cargo or even on the most vagabond of old tubs, there is always a fine coffin, often luxurious, that is not meant for passengers but which belongs to the members of the crew working on the E.S.R.

The E.S.R. is not a political group per se, although many registered ships, including the reddest ones, form part of it. It is an association of seamen whose purpose is to guarantee its adherents a return to their native land and a decent burial in case of death during a cruise or while in a foreign port.

The E.S.R. is, in short, an anti-burial-at-sea league. It is successful because no group is more sentimental than people of the sea. Its adherents include the navigators, old seadogs and the seamen who have vagabonded their entire life. Even the most adventurous and reckless among brainless seamen or pilots who have the travel itch and are revellers regularly pay their fees to this brotherhood. It is responsible for getting them back to their loved ones, to the cemetery of the village where they are native, and for whom the initials E.S.R., far from being mysterious, are a marvellous promise that allows them to dream since the initials mean: "You are leaving, but you shall return!"

Thus, on board the Saint-Wandrille, this hilarious practical joker and this old comedian of a Bordelais who never gave a thought to the world, and had the malice to not believe in God or the devil, and whose elevated spirit was always ready for a bit of mischief and to laugh at the next man, was during his lifetime, the most ardent propagandist and adherent, the most faithful member of the E.S.R. Any of his money not invested in cratefuls of plonk was spent on adorning the coffin on board. He hadn't hesitated to pay out of his own pocket. He once paid for a tiny mattress to pad the bottom. Then another time, to pad it inside with blue satin, or yet again, exchanging the ordinary handles for sterling silver ones struck with the initials of the brotherhood. He had replaced the casket cover, which was full, by a cover with a one-way mirror so that the coffin of the Saint-Wandrille became an icon for parades, equipped with accessories as numerous as they were luxurious. It was overloaded with pagan decorations placed at angles and on the perimeter: sirens, dolphins, Neptune, goddesses, stars, sun, anchors, shells, all in gilded bronze. Everyone on board talked enviously about the coffin. It outshone the coffins of all the other cargos of the Company. And Jules, Désirée, Bien-aimé, August Quinquenbois, the baker, took the most pride. He ended up considering himself, if not the owner, at the very least as the legitimate guardian of the famous object. And because the mortuary chamber of the Saint-Wandrille was door to door with the oven, when you didn't hear the Bordelais operating his kneader, you found him in the funeral depot, cleaning, polishing or varnishing the large coffin made of ebony wood. You would often see him sanding and polishing the coffin and looking continuously at a casket representing everyone's salvation.

VI

Tightly wound in white tourist bedsheets marked with the monogram of the Company, the head wrapped in bandelettes that dissimulated the horrible incision of the surgeon's knife that had emptied his skull and by which the brain had flowed out, the Bordelais was placed inside the coffin that he had maintained with such care. Now, Tronche, the bosun, was screwing the richly embroidered cover onto him. It was hard to detect the profile of the bloated, blackened face of the baker, buried in funereal lace.

The autopsy, the embalming, and the placing into the casket had been a terrible struggle in the suffocating atmosphere of the oven amidst the ship roll. The three men hurried to get this sad task over and done with.

"Here, the night is falling. But the hardest task remains to be accomplished, don't you think, doctor?" the steward said to Marcelin. "We still have our reports to write. And if you cannot mention all the tattoos that this bastard had on his skin, then by what right can I announce that he was dead drunk when he died? But do I at least have the right to give some particulars? Oh, la, la, that won't be too convenient with the Company! I don't want to shame his family when they have to attend the offices to have his remains and retrieve his gear. Ah, you see some hilarious ones in the marine! Tell me, Tronche, when you throw this into the water (the steward had just reached for a pail containing the gut and brain of the deceased), you can come to my cabin for the inventory. Bring his bag and his suitcase. And you have to be there. I need a witness. It's in the regulations."

But neither the steward nor the doctor answered Verdier. Increasingly ill at ease, Marcelin took his distance on his wooden clogs, his toolbox hanging from the shoulder, and the bloody pail rattling at the end of his arms.

"It smells funny here," Verdier said, lighting a cigarette. "Are you coming?"

The two officers departed, closing the door carefully.

But before taking leave of each other at the end of a corridor, the steward tapped on the shoulder of the doctor:

"Don't worry, my friend. If you are embarrassed by your report, maybe by looking around, I can find some autopsy minutes in the old ship papers. You can use them as a model. See you later, all right?"

Outside, the wind had died down, but the sea was still heavy. When the propeller of the Saint-Wandrille turned into the emptiness, the vibrations of the main shaft transmitted to all the ship's surfaces before the cargo fell again heavily and was now topsy-turvy.

From his post, the electrician leaned on a lever, and all the lights on board lit up simultaneously.

At the salon, a small boy leafed carefully through a book of images.

At the bar, the laughs and the glasses clashed with each other. We were on the cusp of arrival within forty-eight hours.

VII

The next day, at the switch of the shift, Tronche ordered two men to descend with them to the oven and to transport the coffin to the neighbouring room. Verdier had announced to him the previous evening that he was coming in early in the morning to inspect the seals on the mortuary chamber's door.

Tronche was a taciturn brute. Nevertheless, when leaning to weigh the coffin, he noticed the face of the man against the one-way glass. Without any regard, he glanced under the cover. Tronche suddenly reared backwards.

"My god!" he said, "Look. You'd think that Bordelais wants to get out of his monument!"

The two seamen hurried. They couldn't believe what they were seeing. The Bordelais' bloated face blocked the window, and his nose was flattened against the glass.

"Do you think it's going to break?" said one.

"You can see that he's moving," said the other.

Indeed, the face of the dead man, with little somersaults that were not due to the rocking of the ship and that we no longer noticed for some time, all of us being transfixed by this disfigured face. Small cracks, as if one could follow with the naked eye, the progressive action of the swelling, working internally, pushing him, pressing him, making him crush himself more and more against the sheet of glass.

"I'm telling you, it's going to burst," one of the seamen said after a moment.

"You're nothing but numbskulls," Tronche replied. "It's his gases that turn him. And then, it's too hot here. Let's get moving; we'll put him on his side, and he'll still be poorly."

So, the three men grabbed the casket and carried it into the tiny enclave that was being used as a mortuary chamber. They had a fair bit of trouble since the doorways were narrow, and it wasn't easy to turn this long box in the corridor without having to tilt it or turn it upside down. Even with three of them, the magnificent coffin was too heavy. Finally, they managed without shaking it up, protecting the fine plating, and they returned to work. But soon the entire deck knew that the Bordelais was moving from inside the coffin, and everybody ran to it, from the fo'c'sle, the lazarette or the deck, to witness the phenomenon. The ship's boy reported this to the bridge, and the second, who was on shift, warned the doctor and the steward.

VIII

When Verdier came out of his cabin, the sky was incandescent pink, and the ocean, although crested with foam, was like soot against this luminous backdrop. During the night, the wind had picked up. A strong breeze from the South was shifting the smoke downwards on the bridge of the Saint-Wandrille, but the waves still broke by the rear.

Tronche, who watched the steward at the entrance of a passage-way, cut off his path.

"I must tell you, chef, that the Bordelais isn't keeping tranquil, and the casket could crack any moment now."

"Are you out of your mind? And what the hell is this story any-way? Oh, la la."

"Come see for yourself.

And the steward tugged Verdier along while explaining to him.

"I'm telling you that this is not a suitable coffin. I bet that this music box won't last. It's filled with plating, but it won't hold, you know ...

There was a crowd in the mortuary room where the heat had become intolerable due to the proximity of the oven that continued to roar behind the partition. The men who wanted to see moved down the corridor in front of the door. Verdier had to elbow his way through to be able to enter the small morgue where a candle had been lit.

The doctor was already there.

Armed with an oversized vaporizer, Marcelin was disinfecting the room's air where a slight, nauseating odour was spreading, sweet, of camphor and rot.

"What is that smell?" Verdier asked.

"Who knows?" Marcelin replied. "He already stinks, and he's puffed out."

"Is there a crack?" the steward asked Tronche, who, having fallen to his knees with his nose on the cashbox, examined the coffin while banging it with his finger.

"I don't know," replied Tronche. "I haven't found anything, and that strikes me as better than I first thought possible, but I don't trust it; you never know, but it's still riddled with flaws. All these things in gold are perhaps plating to conceal defects in the wood. There is maybe a hole in the box."

"A hole in the box!" a mechanic standing at the threshold shouted. But ours is the finest coffin that has ever navigated. You're speaking nonsense, bosun; you know well that the Bordelais was always in the act of refitting his cabin. He was more caulker than baker! Ah, you can always throw him in the water; it'll float, this huge box. Take it from me."

"Maybe it's what is going to happen," Verdier said. "We can't keep that thing on board."

These words unleashed the anger of the men present.

"What?"

"What are you saying?"

"You're going to toss him in the water?"

"But this is a scandal!"

"Come now, he's one of the brotherhood, the Bordelais, you aren't ..."

"We're not thinking of sticking the Maccabeans behind the bread oven!"

"You can see they have never navigated, the engineers. It's the same old—always buggering up!"

"What bastards!"

"It's always the same drinking the champagne."

"So, the Company doesn't give a damn about us, right?"

"All they care about are the shareholders."

"You're going to shovel him overboard? No way!"

"The Bordelais has to come home with us. We'll give him a proper burial. What do you say, men?"

"Jules was one of the E.S.R.!"

The protestations were unanimous and getting increasingly vehement.

Seeing it was early morning, they were all there: those in blue, the stokers and those in striped jerseys, and also those in aprons, the cook, the butcher, the storage man, the new baker's boy and the maître d' and the waiters in shirt-sleeves, all of them protesting at the thought that we would consider tossing this special coffin overboard and along with it their good old boy Jules. Désiré. Bienaimé.

Auguste Quinquembois, who had spent so much money on this monument, would perhaps never see his native land.

"And what do you want me to do, then?" Verdier said. "We can't conserve him on board. There's no getting around the regulation. Do you feel like catching cholera?"

But the protests sprang up anew, and the steward started seriously to be chided by the indignant crew when the butcher lifted his fist, took a step forward and shouted:

"Calm down, comrades! I've got an idea ..."

Big Fernand, the butcher, enjoyed a certain authority on board due to his prodigious physical strength.

"Commissaire," he said, scratching his nape, "Commissaire ... we aren't going to lose such a beautiful coffin that cost us so much money? Since the Bordelais keeps moving around in the coffin, why don't we stick him in the fridge?"

But the steward shrugged his shoulders.

"Come, doctor, we will talk with the Captain."

And Verdier left on that note.

He was furious.

"Blockheads, *va*—a gang of idiots," he thought.

And he consoled himself.

"What a Company!"

IX

Captain Delademeure didn't like the unexpected.

He was a cordial, kind man and even a bon vivant.

But he was very proud of piloting the Saint-Wandrille, the most modern cargo of the Company, a beautiful boat of fifteen thousand tons. He hoped to nail down a command on the New York line. He was well known at the Company, where his progress up the ladder had been one of the most rapid in the postwar period. So, his ambition was no longer limited, and all hopes were allowed. Worldly, engaging tale-teller, inexhaustible dancer, both respectful and charming, he was a star in the eyes of his passengers because this forty-two-year-old Captain had indisputable charisma and elegance—a fine piece of officer.

But according to tradition—and contrary to the English, who were entirely oriented towards questions of service, and the Germans, where circumstances do not always justify the morgue (in every degree)—the headquarters of a French long courier seemed to attach honour to one's weighty responsibilities and the daily technical tasks. Captain Delademeure did not have the airs of someone in the service of the Company when he conducted himself as courteous and attentive master of the house vis-à-vis passengers. Yet officers on board knew how hard, curt, and even harsh the "old man" could be for a minor act of negligence or fault in service.

Captain Delademeure displayed his authority and savoir-faire at the burial-at-sea of a certain Quinquembois. Any seaman worthy of the name is also a diplomat. It is often more challenging to soothe an unhappy and overworked crew than to pilot a ship that has driven into a storm.

X

As soon as he heard about the morning incidents, Captain Delademeure harshly rebuked his agent and doctor, who had informed him. He reproached Verdier for his lack of sang-froid and inconsiderate remarks that—after having brought the men forward, then treating them as pig-headed, which was highly clumsy, and Marcelin, with his inexperience, his recklessness, his culpable negligence for having allowed the baker's coffin to "cook all night in front of the oven." Then, he convened his bosun, the heads of the various on-board services, a delegation of six crew members, two representatives of the "E.S.R.," then Fernand, the butcher and Emile, the ship's boy.

"Tronche," he said, once everybody was gathered in the card room, "take care to provide for the quarter-deck. To starboard. The

Eastern wind is rising. I foresee things improving in the evening, and the ceremony can occur. I have given my orders to the second. Go see him."

And thus, from the outset, marking his authority, the Captain addressed the men surrounding him as follows:

"My friends, I am sorry to announce the death of your dear comrade, Jules. Désiré. Bien-Aimé. August Quinquembois, baker of the Saint-Wandrille, a faithful servant of the Company, died in the line of duty, carrying out his duty throughout this ferocious equinox storm we have just suffered. The burial-at-sea of this worthy worker shall take place this evening, during the third shift, as I have just ordered."

And turning towards the ship's boy:

"You, Emile, will carry out my command. I have designated you to do the service to the halyard for the salute of the flag. It's a dangerous assignment. The sea is high. But you have well deserved an honour in this affair."

Then, addressing the gathered assembly: "For there is, it appears, a Bordelais affair? It would appear that the deceased is 'tossing and turning in his sleep.' The doctor gave me his report. Your comrade is dead of blood to the head. He was embalmed to be able to bring him back to France. But, voilà, his brain proved not to be watertight, and it was too hot. Under these conditions, we cannot keep him on board without the danger of an epidemic, nor can we disembark him tomorrow in Havana without being quarantined, which would consequently trigger new delays, and we would suffer a plethora of interruptions and interference for the Company and our passengers, not to mention the fact that not a single man on board could disembark, as you all know the severity of the authorities in Cuba. That's why I have ordered the burial at sea ceremony to occur shortly before our arrival in the island's territorial waters. Have I acted correctly?"

And taking the butcher aside, who had remained utterly perplexed, Captain Delademeure said to him in a familiar tone:

"To be sure, in your suggestion to put the Bordelais in the fridge, there is an idea of merit ... but this idea is impossible to carry

out. You have not considered the wrong that would be inflicted
upon the Company and the good name of France if this story were
to go public. If the news spreads to our foreign competitors that we
store cadavers inside our food freezers, we might as well be admit-
ting we're keeping corpses in the pantry! You can well understand
that this is impossible. We won't have a single traveller on the line,
and we have to defend our flag today more than ever because the
times are difficult for us. I promise I will intervene personally with
the Company so that we can be given another cabin, for example,
behind the nursing station, because you are right, there's plenty of
room on board."

And then, turning towards the two representatives of the
brotherhood: "Now, one other thing. I want to say a word on the
coffin of the E.S.R. Like you, I regret the loss of such a precious
object for members of the Fraternity on board. Not to mention the
deceased, who devoted all his savings to embellishing it, maintained
it jealously and with the most extraordinary devotion. Such a beautiful piece should not be lost, nor should we forget the virtue of such
a brave man. I would therefore ask you to perpetuate his memory on
board, to add your names at the top of the list for the purchase of a
new coffin as beautiful as the present one—and I believe that the
steward and the doctor also fervently desire to participate in this
homage by each registering for the sum of one hundred francs.
Further, I will pass the hat to our passengers after the ceremony. I do
not doubt that this initial capital once collected will facilitate the
task of realizing the humanitarian purpose that the E.S.R. is pursuing—and we owe it to posterity to keep a stiff upper lip despite the
difficulties and the fatality, and honour the promise registered in his
noble maxim and engraved in the heart of each seaman with love for
his country: 'You depart, but you shall return!'

"Does anyone have any objection to make or anything else to
propose?"

And since no one responded, he said, after allowing a moment
to pass and pulling his prayer book out of his pocket: "All right, follow
me. I will now bid our friend adieu."

XI

The final stage of the crossing went better. The weather improved, and the ceremony remained very moving in its simplicity. The burial on the high seas proved dignified and memorable, allowing numerous passengers to take interesting, instant photos. The collection had also proved fruitful. In summary, this painful story, which could have gone awry, ended in the best possible result and for once, Verdier was happy, for, contrary to his habit, he had no difficulty in drafting his report, having had the idea to use the phrases of the Captain during his harangue: "a worthy employee," "a faithful servant of the Company," "died in the line of duty," to announce the death of the baker that otherwise he would have been unable to report to the front office without fearing an assignment of blame as a result of exposing himself and his crew to unforeseeable complications. Everything had turned out all right.

"Ah, 'the old man,' what a man. He really pulled one over on us, me and the doctor, said the steward, slipping the papers that he had just put together inside a large envelope that he had addressed to the headquarters of the Company. Then, he dipped his pen into the inkwell and filled out the following shipping certificate:

SHIPPING CERTIFICATE		
No	DEEDS	Stamp of receipt
Death Certificate Qinquembois (Jules Désiré. Bienaimé. Auguste).		
Embalming Report		
Minutes of immersion		
Steward's report		
Inventory of personal belongings of deceased		

Then, he dated the certificate: "On board the Saint-Wandrille, 29 March 1936" and signed his initials.

Finally, he rubbed his hands with contentment and drew his blotter from a drawer and the photo of his wife that he had found in the pocket of the dead man.

"Shameless tart, "he said, "but I still love you …"

And he lit a cigarette and went out on the bridge.

The pilot's flagship approached.

The port of Havana shimmered in the distance.

The flag of the Company flew at half-mast, and further down at the horn, the blue square and the yellow square for the application for a visitor's visa processed by the port authorities and the medical service delivered free-of-charge by the state.

XII

The Saint-Wandrille had already made two or three new voyages from Le Havre to Vancouver, crossing the Panama Canal on both ends of the return trip. Nobody on board thought anymore about the Bordelais and the sad fate that had befallen him. Then, one day, at the Cristobal stopover, the Company agent in Colon boarded the cargo vessel and delivered a heavy envelope from the front office in Paris to the Captain.

Captain Delademeure had barely cast a glance at the letter accompanying the sending that this sociable man spewed out a curse and sent Marius, the first mate, to find the steward with an order to come urgently and to bring along the file on the late baker, Quinquembois.

"Monsieur!" roared the Captain as soon as Verdier presented himself with the file under his arm. "Monsieur, read this and explain yourself. We have been fined ten thousand dollars. I am bearing the blame. And you are also accountable for a pair of bedsheets you have stolen. Ah, you're a fine one!"

And the Captain, under the eyes of the stunned purser, displayed the letter from the front office, with the main excerpts highlighted in blue.

Paris, 11 November 1936, departmental letter 16.742.Co
Company headquarters to the Captain of the Saint-Wandrille

Please take note of the court report of the American authorities for-
warded by our Counsel in New York, a copy of which is herewith.
You will note pursuant to this report that:

1° A coffin hit land, washed in on Miami Beach (Florida) on
    1 April 1936 at 7:00 am;
2° said coffin, decorated with mythological themes in gilded copper,
    was intact and appeared in mint condition, which leads us to the
    conclusion that it had not sojourned for long in the water;
3° the handles in silver of said coffin were struck with the following
    initials: E.S.R.;
4° once opened, in the presence of a justice of the peace and the
    Miami coroner, the coffin contained the corpse of a man, clearly
    a seaman based on his tattoos, recently deceased and who had
    undergone surgical intervention "post-mortem" in contempla-
    tion of an embalmment;
5° said cadaver of the seaman was enveloped in new bedsheets of
    tourist quality, marked with the monograms of the Company,
    which allowed for the conclusion that this anonymous corpse,
    without an identity plate, had no other distinctive signs other
    than his tattoos in French. It appears that said corpse was buried
    at sea by a ship belonging to the Company during a crossing in
    late March off the coast of Florida.
6° according to a tattoo (which was challenging to decode due to its
    age and undertaken by incision of the belly), the aforementioned
    unknown seaman is named Robert Durnand or Dournand or
    Dournour;
7° said coffin contained no ballast inside, nor traces of ballast out-
    side, or the ballast was poorly stowed;
8° due to a violation of international regulations and American
    shipping decrees prohibiting the immersion of a body in territor-
    ial waters, the Company is hereby ordered to pay a fine in the
    amount of 10,000 dollars.

After our investigation and research on the subject of the man who washed up on the Miami shoreline and identified as belonging to the Company, based upon the sheets that enshrouded him, sheets of tourist class, and that bore our mark, it can only be that of Quinquembois (Julys, Désiré, Bienaimé, Auguste) deceased on board the Saint-Wandrille. You had announced the immersion in your maritime report, dated March 29, 1936. No other unit of the Company was navigating in these waters at the relevant time.

Upon these grounds and due to the negligent approach to the immersion and the disorder that appears to reign in the services on board the Saint-Wandrille, the Company imputes blame upon the Captain and the steward, who disposed of a pair of sheets without establishing an outgoing corresponding chit and without replacing them, and for which the steward remains accountable vis-à-vis the Company.

But doubt exists, as your shipping report contradicts in several points the observations made by the authorities of Miami. Please advise us in your reply to this report:

a) the exact point of immersion;
b) why the coffin was not weighted as prescribed by law and regulations;
c) how a coffin immersed into the sea off the coast of Cuba could land three days later on a Miami beach (Florida)?
d) how the Miami authorities could record the presumed names of the deceased as Robert Durnand or Dournand or Dournour, names that appear on no list of the Company, nor in any roll from 1900 to 1936?

We draw your attention to this last point, which may permit the Company to appeal the judgment of Miami and be exempted from payment of the fine you have been ordered to pay. For this purpose, you are invited to surrender to a rigorous investigation on board to determine whether you cannot trace the disappeared baker or whether the so-called Robert Durnand or Dournand or Dournour wasn't a stowaway.

From the management
Signed: illegible

N.B.—on the issue of the tolerance granted by the Company to the members navigating the E.S.R. to embark a coffin belonging to them, as of this day, the Company will solely agree to the boarding of coffins made of lead.

(Notice—to be posted)

"Oh la la, what a story!" Verdier said, crushed. "The Company ..."

"Enough!" the Captain said. "Enough of your ravings. It's not the season. Do you think I won't accept the blame they want to inflict upon me—any more than the fine? Come on, steward, explain yourself."

"But, Captain, what do you want me to tell you? I don't understand. I am crushed. What sheets are they talking about? I never stole anything. It's the office that has something against me. I can promise you that I never wanted to lead you to think that we put the Bordelais in his coffin. It was painful. We were in a rush. I don't recall. It is possible that ..."

"Come now, Verdier, calm down. We are not going to start acting like the front office. We will respond, *que diable*, and put them in their place. Can you see that? I have to find the baker. A certificate of death duly executed will not suffice. Now—and what are they making of my signature? But I will put half of the crew on hold, have the bunkers dusted, sift through the ashes in the oven, take samples of sweepings and send them to Paris for analysis. I give you my word that this affair is not terminated and that I'm going to make life difficult for them. So, they want paperwork, all right then, I'll give it to management! And to start, you will give me the pleasure, commissaire, of drawing up a detailed inventory of the linen room and don't forget anything, not even the rags. So, a pair of bedsheets is on board, and there is mayhem and chaos everywhere."

Captain Delademeure was indignant. But shortly after, he returned to the topic:

"Tell me, Verdier, in your opinion, is it the coffin of Quinquembois that ran aground in Miami?"

"Oh, of that, Captain, there is no doubt. The coffin of the Saint-Wandrille was unique in the merchant marine. Look at the judge's report. It was an idea of the Bordelais. He didn't have another one. I recognize it. It's ours."

"Well, why wasn't it ballasted?" the Captain asked.

"But, Captain, it was so heavy that seven men were barely sufficient to carry it up to the bridge. Never in my life did I dream that it would float. Do you recall the sea raging? Everybody thought there was a hole in the ship. Do you recall a terrible odour? I was convinced that the ship would sink. The box wasn't watertight."

"It's true. I recall we did it quickly because there was terrible weather, and everybody was exhausted. But we should have been careful because you can never take enough precautions with the sea and because this joker of a Bordelais who was always busy with his coffin must have been a famous caulker. But you're not responsible for that, Verdier. It's the second time I've been in charge of a burial at sea, and it had been decided it was unnecessary to ballast the coffin because it was so heavy. Still, it's unheard of that he could turn up on the coast of Florida. There was a famous wind from the East that day, and of course, the sea was filled with currents; nevertheless, I cannot believe that this character had found his way to Miami. No, do you see our Quinquembois sculling?"

"Maybe it was his gas that kept him afloat."

"Ah, do you think so? I always thought that our young doctor botched up the embalming. It's too bad he's no longer on board. I would be curious to have his opinion. By the way, what is this tattoo? Durand, Dournant, Robert Dournour that he had on the belly?"

"Oh la la! He had tattoos everywhere, Captain. I recall telling Marcelin that he couldn't remove them all, or the report could have been a whitewash. I am not saying that, my Captain, and you know he was rather timid, our young doctor."

"What then?"

"But this tattoo on the belly ... oh, la ... but they are funny, these Americans ah! ... But Captain, Robert Durand, Dournant, or Robert Dournour, what you have just said, but it's ..."

"It's?"

"Well, yes ... Imagine that the Bordelais had a tattoo on the belly around the pubis, and that was not easy to decode due to all the hair. Oh, la la! ... but it's crazy. What a Company ... Robert Durnour ... It's Robinet d'amour[2] that you have to read ... That's who it is ... Quinquembois!"

XIII

Four days later, the Saint-Wandrille left the port of Havana. The coast of Cuba started to recede in the wake when the second, who was on shift, saw Captain Delademeure climbing onto the bridge.

"Justin," the Captain said, "Pay attention. I want to locate the exact point where the Bordelais was immersed because the story concerns me. Did you know what I calculated? Buried at sea on March 29 during the evening in these waters and landed the 1st of April in the morning in Miami, that's an average of 5 knots. Ah, the bugger, it's unbelievable."

"Indeed, Captain, it's beyond imagination. But what amazes me is that he came back."

"How so, came back?"

"Well, yes, Captain, according to the promise of the E.S.R.: *Exeatis Sed Revertemur. You depart today but shall one day return!*

---

2. Phallus of love.

Acknowledgements

To:

The late Miriam Cendrars, Blaise Cendrars' daughter, for letting me trample in her secret garden.

The late Jean-Paul Caracalla, for those lunches at Aux Deux Magots.

Olivier Rubinstein, former DG at Editions Denoël, for leaving a place for the unwashed in the Denoël stable.

Joe Hartlaub, for giving me the hard-boiled seal of approval.

Chloé, for listening to my doggerel day-in and out.

Liam, for his loyalty, nobility and ferocious courage.

Michael Mirolla, for his infinite patience and for believing in Cendrars.

Jim Christy, for a life worthy of Cendrars and for keeping the bums, vagrants and vagabonds in the loop. For still hitting the road, wherever it leads.

Z, for her wisdom of the heart.

God, for wresting me back from the precipice more times every day than I can count.

About the Author

LIKE HIS CONTEMPORARY Picasso, who also appeared to be locked in mortal combat with the tsunami of modernity, Blaise Cendrars' kaleidoscopic lives can be viewed through the lens of successive periods, each of which mark Cendrars' merging of art and life so radically, that the more he revealed, the more he appeared unfathomable, enigmatic and extraordinary.

Cendrars was born Frédéric Sauser to a sickly Anabaptist mother and a failed inventor of a father. By age 15, he is already a runaway, his choice of destination random and his vehicle of choice the train, taking him through Germany, onwards to St Petersburg, Russia, where he works as a jeweller, discovers the Imperial Library, witnesses the Tzars' Guards shoot into a crowd of demonstrating citizens on Russia's Bloody Sunday in 1905, and first picks up a pen to compose poetry. He later travels along the Trans Siberian route by rail, selling coffins and knives and jewels, finds his way to New York and conjures up his epic poem, "Easter in New York", that hits the turgid world of French poetry like a hurricane, starting his own review, *Les Hommes Nouveaux*. In 1911, he publishes "Prose of the Transsiberian", his epic, Homerian saga of his adventures in Russia on 2 metre pages, illustrated by Sonia Delaunay. When placed end-to-end, the

150 pages are the same height as the Eiffel Tower. The poet vagabond has burst onto the Paris literary scene, like his contemporaries
Chagall, Léger, Modigliani, and his old carnie pal, Charlie Chaplin.
He develops a technique in his Kodak series of poems, where each
poem is a "snapshot".

The poet turns warrior at the outbreak of World War I, and
then the inevitable cataclysm, as he is wounded by German machine
gunfire, and loses his right arm.

Cendrars elects his strategy of choice—fugue—finding refuge
with the tziganes, and peace of mind in the tranquil village of
Tremblay-sur-Mauldre, where he is now buried.

In 1918, Cendrars buries his past with "I have killed", describing
his killing of a German soldier, and moves on, as writer and man,
ready to mine the vein of the horrors he has endured, and the men
he has crossed.

He emerges as Cendrars the novelist, charting adventures and
political scandals with the international best-sellers *Gold, Rum,
Hollywood* and *Dan Yack*. These are tales of adventure, greed and
corruption. *Moravagine*, the tale of a serial killer, is another seismic
event, not only a prophecy, but a diatribe against the corruption of
culture by psychiatry. Cendrars is moulding a new style, literary
reportage, in a hard-boiled version evocative of James Ellroy, writing
on Hollywood, Basque people smugglers, the Marseilles mob as an
insider who frequented these milieux.

While the Paris literary scene degenerates into movements and
sub-movements, Cendrars moves on, takes his literary and physical
distance, crosses the ocean to Brazil, becomes one of the prime mov-
ers in samba becoming Brazil's national music.

In the late 1930s, Cendrars crosses another Rubicon, and writes
a series of *True Tales*, commissioned by Paris-soir, where the real life
adventurer becomes the first-person narrator of the adventures he is
describing. Cendrars the adventurer and Cendrars raconteur are now
one and the same.

In 1939, while preparing to sail around the world, war breaks
out and Cendrars becomes a war correspondent. When France falls,

he resorts once again to fugue. There is no truth, only action. He disappears to Aix-en-Province behind a wall of self-imposed silence. For three years. Reborn again after the war, retaking his position at his Remington N° 1 Portable at age 56, he produces some of his best work. At its nexus, a story of his life and times as self-portrait, in a spectacular triptych: *Bourlinguer* (*Vagabond*), *Le Lotissement du Ciel* (*The celestial subdivision*) and the *Severed Hand*. The prose is torrential, rhythmic, musical, and the energy is driven by atavistic blood and violence.

Adventurer, poet, interpreter of modernity, precursor of Marshall McLuhan, soul mate of Robert Graves and Erich Maria Remarque, Blaise Cendrars fearlessly sought out the ultimate sense of life beyond appearances, and one forged through action. He frequently expressed an enormous compassion for the suffering of the ordinary man.

Blaise Cendrars died on January 21, 1961. Yet another fugue. And, behind him, as with the great Chinese ascetics, his personal thoughts are unknown to us, only his aphorisms and his koan-like observations, dropped like a thousand petals in late Spring. A man whose imagination and lust for the world could not be quenched, an ascetic whose message is contained in the following words:

"Only a soul full of despair can ever attain serenity and, to be in despair, you must have loved a good deal and still love the world."

About the Translator

DAVID J. MACKINNON spent the first 19 years of his life in exile in British Columbia, the land of his birth, and has since found refuge variously in Hong Kong, Montreal, Paris, and Amsterdam. MacKinnon wrote a novel on Blaise Cendrars, *The Eel* (Guernica, 2016), and translated a series of 1950 France Télévisions interviews, titled *Blaise Cendrars Speaks* (Ekstasis Editions, 2016). He is currently preparing Volume II of Cendrars' *True Tales* and a novel, *Who carries this carcass down the road?*

About the Editor

PATRICK KEENEY'S WRITINGS have appeared in a wide variety of journals in the scholarly and popular press in Canada, the UK, and the U.S. He is the author of *Liberalism, Communitarianism, and Education: Reclaiming Liberal Education.* He divides his time between Kelowna, B.C., and Thailand.

MIX
Paper
FSC® C100212

Printed by Imprimerie Gauvin
Gatineau, Québec